Write Michigan 2024-2025 Anthology

Chapbook Press

Chapbook Press
Schuler Books
2660 28th Street SE
Grand Rapids, MI 49512
616.942.7330
www.schulerbooks.com

ISBN 9781966196181

Janyre Tromp   **Kate Messina**
Susan Morrel-Samuels **Natalie Koepke**
Abbie Pedrotte   **Lorna Garlets**
Alexander Davidson   **Liliana Harkema**
Edward Burkhead   **Frank Yanover**
Max Bufkin   **Addison Craig**
Vicki Berger Paulissen **Frances Heethuis**
Sophia Constance Wegner **Kayla Simons**
Zak Burns   **Jesca Westra**
Joyce Tchuente

Printed in the United States by Chapbook Press.

Table of Contents

Foreword
By Janyre Tromp ix

Adult Judges' Choice Winner
Serina by Susan Morrel-Samuels 1

Adult Judges' Choice Runner-Up
Something About Him by Abbie Pedrotte 8

Adult Readers' Choice Winner
A Place at the Table by Alexander Davidson 16

Adult Published Finalists
Forty Autumns by Edward Burkhead 24
Yellow Eyes in a New World by Max Bufkin 31
Blue Star Mother by Vicki Berger Paulissen 38

Teen Judges' Choice Winner
Three-Legged Race by Sophia Constance Wegner 45

Teen Judges' Choice Runner-Up
A Road to Travel by Zak Burns 51

Teen Readers' Choice Winner
Some Things That We Hide by Joyce Tchuente 58

Teen Published Finalists
Passenger Planes and Burning Buildings by Kate Messina 63
Music by Natalie Koepke 72
The Cow That Jumped Over the Moon by Lorna Garlets 78

Youth Judges' Choice Winner
Safe by Liliana Harkema 86

Youth Judges' Choice Runner-Up

Is this real? by Frank Yanover 93

Youth Readers' Choice Winner

The Pirate Cove's Treasure by Addison Craig 99

Youth Published Finalists

Suicide Hotline, Make The Call by Frances Heethuis 107

The Present by Kayla Simons 114

A Friend to Follow by Jesca Westra 121

About Write Michigan 125

2025 Judges 127

Acknowledgments 130

Sponsors 132

Schuler Books Self-Publishing Services 133

Foreword

By Janyre Tromp

I was in kindergarten the first time I published an award-winning story. Well, kind of.

1. I did write a short story in kindergarten. It was about a duck I'd seen in the pond by my house. He was diving for food . . . and I don't remember much beyond that.
2. Our school did print all the stories and bind them. But a spiral-bound mimeograph is hardly published, is it?
3. And the duck story won an award for my grade.

So technically, I won an award, and at the time I was excited. But the paper certificate was quickly lost and no one remembered my award the next year when I didn't win. Others wrote far better than I did, and my little story was hardly high literature, nothing worth remembering year after year, right?

After that start, I hung up my pen and satiated my love of Story by reading anything I could get my hands on. After all, I wasn't a real writer, was I? I hadn't won an Edgar, wasn't a New York Times Bestseller, I was . . . nothing. For quite a while, the only stories I told were to the animals who wandered the forest with me, untethered from the reality of school and home. But I continued to be a voracious reader. I read *The Lion, the Witch, and the Wardrobe* in first grade and then proceeded to plow through any book I could get my hands on. As I settled into the humdrum cement walls of middle and then high school, I turned my attention to the sciences . . . chemistry, to be specific. I was curious about how the world works, how to defeat disease, and, if I'm honest, it's fun to blow things up.

I started college as a chemistry major, hoping to get into research and explore all the nooks and crannies that fascinated me. It took me exactly three months to realize that I hated all the formulas, the facts, and the exacting precision. Even my professor accidentally melting the sidewalk while smelting iron couldn't revive my passion. I called my mom, completely at a loss for what to do. She told me to "do what you love." I, in all my seventeen-year-old wisdom, said, "No one gets paid to read, Mom!"

We'll pause here to say: Pay attention to your mom, kids. They really do know what they're talking about. As a book editor, I am, for all intents and purposes, paid to read. Moms are almost always right.

Anyway, I declared an English major and a communications minor and floundered about for what I was going to do with my life. At the same time, I took the required U.S. history class. In a classroom ringed by the U.S. presidents, I fully expected to be bored out of my gourd with the typical collection of random dates about people who died long before my memory, doing amazing things that I could care less about.

However, Dr. Jones took a different tactic and gave us an assignment that changed my trajectory. The assignment? Go talk to a family member about WWII, the Great Depression, or Korea and write a paper about it.

If I'm honest, I wasn't thrilled about the assignment (was it too late to go blow something up?). But I loved my grandparents and took the opportunity to visit Grandma and Bobpa to talk about their lives. Over glasses of lemonade, I found out how my grandmother went to college during the Depression (with a fur coat, no less) and graduated from Purdue. They told me about the decision for my grandfather to sign up before he was drafted into WWII, thus staving off being shipped overseas. Bobpa eventually became a liaison pilot, of whom seven out of ten didn't come home. In Europe, he dragged around a piano box with a hole in it to use as a portable outhouse. The afternoon instigated a monthly phone call from me to my grandmother where she bequeathed me a host of her other recollections I now have logged in my memory. Every tale they told showed me a different part of who they were and who I am. Stories that told what life was like for them and the mistakes, hopes, and dreams of another generation. Because I loved my grandparents, I loved their stories.

But even more, my grandparent's stories revived my love of telling stories. As I grew older and studied, I realized that my passion for narratives is based in science. Our brains are built to take the facts hiding inside stories and *experience* those facts as if we lived them ourselves. Did you catch that? The tremendous power of Story is that it gives us a relatively safe place to work through life's hardest problems and questions *before* we experience them ourselves. Story helps us map out a better world and better ways to interact with one another. But in my mind, I still wasn't a real writer. Authors were vaunted heroes belonging in the clouds, perhaps sitting on Mount Olympus next to Zeus. There's a power to Story that must be respected. I, surely, was not worthy to hold the responsibility. It wasn't until I'd been working in publishing for almost a decade (getting paid to read) that the managing editor suggested I try my hand at writing. With his nudge I tried it, and the rest, as they say, is history. Kind of.

As many authors will tell you, the authorial road is far from straight or predictable.

The reality is that I wrote a book, published it, and then photographed two board books and published those. And then the publisher stopped publishing those types of books, and I went dormant as a writer again.

Yes, as an editor, I shepherded other people's stories, and I imagined entire worlds with my kids. But I didn't have the brain space to write anything down. Who would want my stories anyway? Despite the power Story held over me, I, like many creatives, could not keep running the marathon without someone kicking me in the proverbial pants to keep me believing that the effort was worth it.

Oh, the mental gymnastics of a creative.

But even if Story hibernates for a time, it seems to crawl from its cave the moment it thinks the time is right. For me, when my kids were both in school full time, I joked to my husband that I should write the next bestselling novel. He told me to try it. And despite the fact I knew the slim odds, I tried it. With my husband's support and my kids sleeping, I spent warm nights on the deck writing, cold evenings in the basement writing, and snippets of time waiting in the pickup line writing. I poured out a book that I loved. And when I was done, I was rejected by agents (those heroes responsible for selling a writer's work) dozens of times. Writers are taught to be persistent, to take in rejection, and to turn out beauty. So I shelved the manuscript and started another book and, in the middle, hit the brick wall called medical emergency. Sitting in a hospital room for months on end is not conducive to writing. Life has a way of forcing writers to experience life more deeply than your average person. After all, a creative's job is to see things others miss and introduce the two. People who take walks with me know I spend half the time crawling into weird places to get a picture of "that cool piece of broken cement." My kids find it weird, but my Instagram followers love it.

As I dug back into the manuscript I'd started, I realized that I'd needed to experience the emotions of a caregiver in order to pass them on to my readers. This lovely phenomenon—reading emotion making us experience emotion—is what boosts fiction readers' ability to recognize others' emotions. It's another superpower of Story: when we read, we learn how to interact and empathize. But the power of Story doesn't stop there. Boston Children's Hospital research proved that reading thirty minutes a day physically rewires our brains, strengthening neural pathways and creating new connections. Our brains literally change with each page. We acquire knowledge, yes. But also curiosity about how other people live and think, about why others do what they do.

Reading allows us to see new dimensions. Then, because of all those lovely connections, regular readers show better memory retention. We gain better storage and recall. In fact, regular readers are drastically less likely to experience cognitive decline. That's right, folks; books fight aging.

A 2009 Sussex University study proved that just six minutes of reading reduces stress by 68%, which is more effective than music (61%) or walking (42%). Imagine what would happen if we walked while we read! Of course, my neighbors think I'm slightly unhinged, but all that stress has to go somewhere! Reading paper books for thirty minutes before bed improves sleep quality and increases REM sleep cycles. I don't know about you, but I'll take better sleep.

Unfortunately writing, like life, isn't easy. There's a reason even the happiest of romances has an "oh no" moment: life is full of "oh no" moments. And if we can find our way through the darkness in the safe space of Story, it helps us build a map for how (or how not) to find the light in real life too.

So as you sit down to read this collection of made-up scenarios and unfamiliar worlds and characters, remember that Story is lending you its superpowers. Lean into the power, enjoy yourself, and then go use your power for good . . . including a helpful nudge to your friendly neighborhood creative.

About the Author

Janyre Tromp is a veteran book editor by day and writer of mid-20th century historical novels with a healthy dose of intrigue and myth at night. She's the award-winning and bestselling author of *Darkness Calls the Tiger, Shadows in the Mind's Eye* and coauthor of both *O Little Town* and *It's a Wonderful Christmas.* And that all happens from her unfinished basement when she's not hanging out with her family, two troublesome cats, and slightly eccentric Shetland Sheepdog. You can find her on social media and her website: www.JanyreTromp.com.

Adult Judges' Choice Winner

Serina
Susan Morrel-Samuels

Serina sat on a plastic chair at a folding table in the stark classroom. She glanced out an open window overlooking the church parking lot. There was no breeze to stir the sticky humid air, and her head itched under her wine-colored scarf. She counted eleven students seated around the tables. Several of the women wore headscarves and long patterned dresses like her own. A young teacher moved from person to person checking their work.

Serina turned her attention to the paper in front of her with a column of numerals and a parallel column of their English names. Her task was to draw lines connecting the numbers with the correct words. The sticks and loops that formed the letters swam in front of her eyes, so different from the flowing Arabic script of her native Pashto. Her thoughts were not in the classroom, but thousands of miles away at her family's home in Afghanistan. They had been her constant preoccupation since she arrived in Detroit with her husband Ahmad six months ago.

She knew she was lucky to have made it out of the country because of Ahmad's work for the Americans. They had been married only a few months before the fall of Kabul. As they squeezed through the chaotic crowds massing at the airport, Serina was in agony because she was leaving behind her mother and younger siblings: two brothers, nineteen and sixteen, and her little sister Fatima, only twelve. Gripping her hastily packed suitcase in one hand and her documents in the other, she was tempted to turn back. If she stepped on that plane, she feared she would never see her family again.

In high school, Serina lost her father to tuberculosis. As the only child old enough to work, she left school to help support the family by sewing. When she turned twenty-one, her uncle arranged a match for her with Ahmad, the son of his good friend. Serina was agreeable to the choice. Ahmad was just two years older, and she knew his sister. His salary from construction work would provide enough money to pay her siblings' school fees and keep the family in food. Now, in America, she and Ahmad needed every penny of the temporary assistance they received.

Serina tried to focus, but her attention kept wandering to the WhatsApp message she'd received that morning from her sister. Fatima texted that their oldest brother, Sayid, had gone to work for the Taliban as a security guard. On one hand, this was good news because it meant some income for the family. On the other, Serina worried that his dealings with the Taliban would affect how he treated their sister. As the oldest male, Sayid was considered the head of the household and the decision maker. Under the Taliban, girls' education ended after sixth grade. Fatima would soon finish her last year of school, and Sayid would dictate her future. Would he allow Fatima to study privately, at home? Would he force her into an early marriage?

A pang of guilt rose in Serina's throat, nearly choking her. When Fatima was born, their mother was consumed with raising two young boys and tending to her ill husband. Serina, at nine, was given responsibility for looking after her tiny sibling. Fatima had taken her first tottering steps into Serina's arms. Her little sister shrieked with laughter when Serina made funny faces, and it was Serina who dried the tears from her glistening brown eyes when Fatima skinned a knee. After Serina married Ahmad and moved to his family's compound, Fatima became so distraught that Serina bought her a cell phone so they could keep in touch daily. She reassured her they would visit each other often. They would always be sisters. And now…

"That's all we have time for today. Thanks for coming. I'll see you again on Thursday."

The teacher's words broke through Serina's dark thoughts like a pebble plunging into a deep well. She gathered her things and rushed to catch the bus. Serina found a seat to herself and rested her head against the cool glass. She was so wrapped in thought she almost missed her stop and hopped off just as the driver was starting to pull away.

Serena climbed the narrow stairs, unlocked her door and entered the hushed, empty living room. Ahmad was still at the restaurant where he washed dishes for cash. The silence bothered her. In Afghanistan, Serina was never alone. Her family's small home was always active and noisy. The densely packed neighborhood was full of people going about their daily routines of shopping and visiting. Smells of cooking wafted through the air at all hours mingled with the sounds of conversation, motorbikes, and the occasional bray of their neighbor's donkey. By contrast, their small apartment felt cavernous and barren.

She went to the bedroom to retrieve a carved wooden box where she kept a few mementos. At the kitchen table, she took out the only photograph of her family. In the image, her father sits on a simple wooden bench with his children grouped on either side. Her mother stands behind him, her black headscarf coiled securely about her neck. Serina observed the deep lines in her father's face and his sunken eyes. The photo was taken just months before his death. His arm is around the thin shoulder of his older son, Sayid, whose face is solemn. Mohammed, three years younger, sits on his left, wearing a mischievous grin. Little Fatima is in Serina's lap, a curl of dark hair on her cheek, bare feet peeking from beneath her dress.

Her mother's brother came to take the picture. Serina, a young teenager at the time, knew her father was ill, but did not realize how serious his condition was. That morning, she picked out her prettiest headscarf, the one with peach-colored flowers. She dressed Fatima and combed her hair. As her uncle prepared to take the photo, she whispered in Fatima's ear that she must stay very still. Now, she envied her younger self, a girl in a flowered scarf who was innocent of all the grief that awaited her.

Tears filled Serina's eyes and spilled down her cheeks. One dripped onto the picture and she wiped it away with her sleeve. When Ahmad entered the apartment an hour later, he found Serina asleep at the table, her head resting on her arms, her fingertips touching the edge of her family's portrait. Ahmad placed a hand gently on her shoulder. She raised her head with a start. For a fraction of a second, she was unsure of where she was.

"Oh, you're home already? I must have fallen asleep." Serina hastily slipped the photo into her box.

"I know how much you miss your family. I miss mine too, but we need to move on with our lives. There is nothing we can do for them until we earn enough money to send back home."

Serina lowered her eyes and clasped her hands in her lap. "Sayid is working for the Taliban. I got a text from Fatima today. I'm so worried – she has no future. There has to be some way to bring her here."

Ahmad shook his head. "The case worker explained it to us. To claim asylum, Fatima would have to go to a third country. She can only travel with a male relative, and even if they had the money, Sayid would never allow it."

"It was selfish to leave; I'm not a good daughter." The tears started to come again, and Serina hastily brushed them away.

"Your mother told you to go. She wanted you to have a better life. You must honor her dream for you."

Serina knew Ahmad spoke the truth, but the guilt she carried was like a torn muscle that throbbed with every step. Try as she might, she couldn't ignore it. She entered the kitchen to put on rice for their meal, reminding herself she should be grateful they had plenty to eat and a safe place to stay.

***

As the months went by, Serina still ached for her family. Every time her phone pinged with a text from Fatima her heart raced. She craved connection, but dreaded bad news. Most of what Fatima wrote was disheartening. Sayid's job was not bringing in enough to get by. Their mother was showing signs of the tuberculosis symptoms that doomed their father. Mohammed had started working in a bakery. He earned little, but at least he was able to bring home a few rounds of flat bread. Fatima was no longer in school and could barely leave the house. Serina prayed that something would change so that she could bring her sister to America.

One sunny fall day, a staff member from the refugee agency showed up at their door with a donated sewing machine. Serena was thrilled as she set it up on her kitchen table. She bought several yards of deep blue cloth with sprays of yellow flowers and made herself a new kameez, a long tunic-style dress with matching pants. When she wore it to her English class, she received several compliments from the other women.

"Where did you buy this?" Noor, her classmate, asked. "There's nowhere in this city to get clothes like we wore at home."

"I made it myself. I used to sew for a living, and now I have a machine here."

"Could you make me one? I would pay you."

Serina was thrilled to get such a request from Noor, an older woman with a round, friendly face. Before long, she had several other orders.

Her fragile equilibrium was shattered by another text from Fatima. One of the Talibs that Sayid worked for had offered a generous bride price for Fatima's hand. If Sayid accepted, she would be betrothed to this man until she turned fifteen, at which time she would become his second wife. Fatima pleaded with Serina to intervene with their brother on her behalf.

Serina sent urgent messages to Sayid using every argument she could think of: fifteen was too young to marry; their mother needed Fatima's help in the household; she and Ahmad would send money as soon as they had any left after paying for rent and food. Sayid responded that he was still making up his mind, but that his future as the family's wage earner would be stronger if he was related to his employer by marriage.

Over the next few days, Fatima sent a series of frantic texts. She said that she was so upset she could neither eat nor sleep. Then her messages abruptly ceased. Finally, Serina received a message from Sayid saying that he had taken Fatima's cell phone away because she was too obsessed with it.

On the day this message arrived, Ahmad returned home to find Serina sitting at their table with swollen eyes and disheveled hair. Spread before her were her identity documents and the meagre cash savings they kept hidden in a tin of tea.

"What are you doing, Serina? What's wrong?"

"I have to go to Kabul. Sayid is definitely going to sell Fatima to a Talib. I can't allow this to happen to my sister. It's my fault for leaving."

"Serina, there's no way you can travel to Afghanistan on a couple of hundred dollars, and even if you could, you would never be able to return to this country."

Serina rose from her chair with clenched fists.

"You don't care about Fatima. All that matters to you is your own happiness. How can I stay here knowing my sister faces a life of servitude and abuse? I'll sell my jewelry; I'll borrow money. I'd take her place if I could!"

"What are you saying? I saved you from that life, and now you want to go back? What about our marriage, our plans? Do you care about me so little that you'd prefer to marry a Talib?"

Ahmad grabbed Serina's upper arm, but she wrenched away and ran to their bedroom where she huddled on the bed, knees to her chest. Through her sobs, she heard the front door of their apartment open and slam shut. Serina cried herself to sleep, and when she woke up Ahmad was gone. She was unsure whether he had ever come to bed.

She got up, washed her face, forced herself to dress and took the bus to English class. Once there, she asked Noor if they could talk. Standing outside of the church, Serina unspooled the story of Fatima's betrothal, and how she must find a way to intervene. She asked Noor if she could borrow money for a ticket to Pakistan. From there she would find some way to cross the border.

"Listen, little sister," said Noor, "All of us have families who are suffering. It breaks our hearts, but you will not help by trying to go on a rescue mission. In fact, you would only cause your family more pain because at least they have the consolation of knowing that you will have a better life. You are their glimmer of hope. Sometime in the future they may be able to follow you, and in the meantime, you can make their lives easier by earning money and sending them whatever you can afford."

"That is easy for you to say. You have your two sons with you. I have no one except Ahmad."

"I also have a sister in Afghanistan. She taught mathematics, and her husband was a journalist. Now, she must stay at home. Her husband lost his job. They have three small children. I pray for them constantly, and I hope to live long enough to see them again."

"How can we bear it?"

"We can't. But we can help each other."

***

Serina returned home defeated. She sat with the shades drawn, staring at nothing. She was startled by the sound of a key in the lock as Ahmad came through the door. He was carrying a small white paper bag.

"I brought us some pastries."

"Butter cookies?"

"Yes, I know they're your favorites."

Serina was touched that Ahmad was trying to make amends for his anger of the previous day. Though she had no stomach for sweets, she rose to greet him.

Over tea and cookies, Serina related her conversation with Noor. She felt like weeping, but she had no more tears.

"Yesterday, I could think of nothing but saving my sister. Now, I have to accept that it's impossible. Perhaps I'm a weak person, but I don't see the sense in going on. What for? Just so I can have a nice life?"

"We have to try, Serina. We have no other choice."

In the following days, Serina barely left the apartment. She stopped sewing and didn't attend class. Ahmad sometimes woke at night to find the bed empty and Serina sitting mutely in the dark living room. Although she continued to cook for him, she barely ate herself, and when she did, she found it hard to keep food down.

One morning, Serina saw the familiar white bubble of a text from Fatima, the first one since Sayid confiscated her phone. Fatima wrote that she had agreed to accept the offer of betrothal. She said the money was essential for the family, especially since their mother needed medical care. Fatima told Serina not to worry about her; she still had two years before the marriage. Maybe something would happen before then.

Serina felt numb. She didn't know if Fatima had written the message herself or if Sayid had dictated it, but it didn't matter. It was over; there was nothing more she could do.

After two weeks Serina received a call from her English teacher, who said she missed her in class and was checking to see if everything was alright. Serina gave a vague answer about having to deal with family issues, but she promised she would return soon. Although she had no motivation to continue her studies, she remembered what Noor had said about helping each other. Perhaps if she confided in her friend, it might ease her pain.

The following day, Serina dragged herself to class. She was relieved to see Noor and found a seat beside her. Noor greeted her warmly, but her tone of voice and wrinkled brow conveyed her concern. Serina knew she had lost weight and that there were dark circles under her eyes. Evidently,

Noor could see this too.

At their break, Noor pulled her aside.

"What is happening to you, sister? Have you been unwell?"

"Fatima has accepted the betrothal. This is keeping me up at night. I feel sick to my stomach almost all the time, and I'm exhausted. It's all I can do to make a meal, and then I don't want to eat it."

"Have you seen a doctor?"

"No, I'm too frightened."

"Come with me to the pharmacy after class. Perhaps I can help."

Serina followed Noor to the boxy, brightly lit drugstore. It had a baffling array of aisles crammed with displays of bottles, boxes, and tubes. Noor led her to a section of women's health products. She selected a narrow white box from the shelf and explained in hushed tones what it was and how to use it.

Serina returned home and followed Noor's instructions with shaking hands. When two pink lines appeared in the opening of the plastic rod, a wave of awe swept over her. She sat perfectly still and felt the world shift gears. The simple bathroom, flooded with afternoon light, seemed like a sacred space. When she stood and looked out the small window, she saw towering white clouds scudding across a robin's egg blue sky. The sun was shining for the first time in weeks, or so it seemed to her.

"If Allah wills, we will have a child, and if it is a girl, I will name her Fatima."

About the Author

Susan Morrel-Samuels enjoys writing short stories and children's books. Her story, *Serina*, was inspired by her volunteer work with the refugee resettlement program at Jewish Family Services of Washtenaw County. Throughout her career at the University of Michigan School of Public Health, she focused on community approaches to preventing violence. She is a member of the Chelsea Writers' Workshop.

Adult Judges' Choice Runner-Up

Something About Him
Abbie Pedrotte

On the evening of their fourth date, Helen suspects Harold of being a serial killer.

Before that, she adjusts the sweater draped over her shoulders, pushes open the front door of Phelps Hall, and steps out into the cool evening. Helen buzzes with excitement. She has never been on a fourth date.

Harold has long limbs and dark, greased-back hair. He's worn a nice shirt and slacks to each of their previous dates, but he's more casual tonight in a fitted white polo and Levi's.

Leaning against his car, he stubs out his cigarette as Helen emerges from Phelps Hall, her home for freshman year at Eastern.

Witnesses describe a newer model, '71 or '72 Oldsmobile Cutlass, black in color, speeding away from campus.

Helen descends the steps at the peak of golden hour. The gilded light casts a peachy glow on the changing leaves of the maple trees, and bronze autumn sunlight sets the chrome of Harold's Oldsmobile Cutlass aflame.

The body of EMU sophomore Bernice Valgood was found on campus by two students late last night.

Helen's suspicion flashes like the beacon of a lighthouse: brief but unmistakable, gone in an instant. A lock of wavy hair falls out of place and dances along Harold's temple. She can't stop staring at it.

Authorities are calling him the Eastern Ripper. They say he could be anywhere.

A hand, confident but reserved enough to be respectful, settles onto the small of her back. A kiss on her right cheek leaves her breathless. Every part of her body feels colder after he pulls away, like he takes all the warmth with him. He holds open the door of the car.

The Ripper's reign of terror began at the start of the semester, and Miss Valgood is the third victim. Autopsies list strangulation as the cause of death for all three women.

Teetering on the highest heels she's ever worn, Helen takes the hand Harold offers, slides into the car, and settles into the spotless upholstery, noticing the fresh scent of the recently-detailed interior.

A white male of tall stature, about six-foot-two, was seen exiting the car with the victim that evening. Witnesses say the driver had dark hair and a shaved face. Another witness reports that the man wore black driving gloves.

Helen's roomate Julia has spent every spare moment parked on the couch, listening to the latest gruesome updates on the Ripper, and biting her fingernails. She dropped all of her evening classes and stopped going out. Julia's fervent anxiety is starting to infect Helen.

She jumps at the sound of Harold closing the door.

Authorities say the crimes are connected, committed by one deranged, sadistic individual. His victims have all been female students. They have all been killed on or near campus, all by strangulation.

From the corner of her eye, she catches sight of black gloves draped on the dash, the leather well-worn.

It's the anxiety, Helen. Makes you think irrationally, she reminds herself as he slides behind the wheel. She can't help the warmth blooming on her cheeks as he reaches over and grabs her hand.

The gloves are just gloves, and his Oldsmobile's paint job is common enough to be a clear coincidence. *Think rationally.*

Ypsilanti's water tower comes into view as Harold maneuvers through the streets, taking them further from campus. Still holding her hand, he uses the stop sign on Washtenaw Ave to steal a quick glance over at her.

Helen has been other dates, of course. Robert Watson barely looked at her. Virgil McCrandal didn't pay attention to a single word that came out of her mouth. William Burt told their mutual friend, "Helen is cute, but just a little too *out there* for me."

Harold gives her hand a squeeze, and her heart soars.

Four dates, and he still wants to hold her hand. She hasn't scared him off. She isn't too much for him.

"Any idea what this drive-in is showing?" she asks, desperate to fill the empty space, suddenly startled and even unnerved by how comfortable the silence is with him; like she could bathe in it.

"A bit of a scary one," he admits with a chuckle. "Certainly not one I'd brag to your father about taking you to, but I have a feeling you won't mind." He winks.

"I'm quite a fan of horror, actually."

"I could have guessed that." His words hold captivation and interest. She searches for repulsion but can't find any.

"What is the name of the film?" she asks, despite no longer being able to breathe. "Maybe I've heard of it."

"The Last House on The Left," he recalls. Helen is almost certain that he

has been smiling since the moment he saw her emerge from Phelps.

Perhaps the color of his Oldsmobile and the black leather gloves should render his perma-smile something to fear.

Helen has no room for fear.

Harold drapes an arm over the back of her seat. She worries for a moment that she might faint, but takes a purgative breath, exhaling to clear the sudden tightness in her throat, and pulls herself together instead.

"Wes Craven," she smiles, coaxing faux ease into her voice. "My roommate almost went and joined a convent after reading the synopsis. I thought I'd have to go see it alone."

Harold turns down a desolate country road, sending Helen's heart into the pit of her stomach.

Mary Wilkins, a sophomore accounting student, is the Eastern Ripper's second victim. Investigators believe she was strangled in a nearby patch of elder trees before being dragged to the field where a farmer later discovered her.

"You're in luck, then," he winks. "Tonight is the first showing. I'm not the biggest fan of horror, but they're calling Wes Craven a hit, if not controversial."

"I don't see why it's so controversial." Her words are tentative, a toe to test the temperature of the pool. Harold waits for her to continue, so she does. "If horrible things can happen in real life, someone is bound to make art about it. And I don't think there's anything wrong with appreciating art."

She holds her breath. Harold pulls into the queue of cars waiting to pay the gate attendant and turns to face her, curious contemplation threaded through that pleasant smile.

"I completely agree."

He takes her on a date every weekend after that. The beginning of Helen's first semester is punctuated by his presence, leaving her positively aglow.

As it turns out, Helen isn't unlovable. At least Harold doesn't think so. If she's honest with herself, she can tell that he finds her endearing. She thinks he might really love her; all of her.

A man her mother set her up with once caught her reading the very provocative Modern Witchcraft by Frank Smyth. He called her *"a preposterous embarrassment."*

Harold, Helen learns, has nothing but admiration for her interest in the crude and unladylike. He doesn't balk at what she watches, reads, and listens to. He doesn't force her out of herself and into someone proper and expected. Perhaps he would have read *Modern Witchcraft* with her.

Harold makes Helen feel wanted.

Helen is absolutely smitten.

When he pulls away from their first kiss, he brushes his fingertips over her cheeks and says "I love when your cheeks flush like that."

She buys a new blush she can't afford the next day. It's called Tickled Peach. She swipes some on the following weekend as she gets ready for Harold to pick her up. Her curly hair is wild and undone, and her emerald green dress is silky enough to show every imperfection but still, somehow, fits her like a glove.

The air is chilly, and pale twilight settles over campus as she takes Harold's offered hand and glides down the steps of Phelps Hall. A wave of timidness washes over her, and she smooths her dress down anxiously, wondering if it's too much. If *she's* too much.

His voice erases every worry.

"I fear you may be the death of me." He wears a smirk that make Helen's knees wobble.

When he bends down to kiss the back of her hand, her skin flushes despite the chill in the air.

The same Oldsmobile Cutlass was seen in the northwest section of campus the night of the Ripper's first kiling. Sources say the maniac's first victim, Karla Goodrow, lived in a dormitory on that side of campus.

They have spent weeks getting acquainted. Every so often, a flash of worry interrupts Helen's pure joy. She feels silly for even giving attention to the suspicion that pesters her.

Harold is not the Ripper because if he was, he would not drive her around in his Oldsmobile Cutlass on the campus he was terrorizing. Helen wouldn't go steady with a murderer, certainly not a stupid one.

Her slight wince at the metallic slam of the car door is barely noticeable, unwarranted; but it is there, unshakable and involuntary, nonetheless.

Miss Goodrow's body was found in some brush only a few hundred yards from the Water Tower. She'd just moved in for her freshman year with plans to study nursing.

Her foot brushes against something on the floor in front of her. She looks down at a length of dirty rope and a stained rag. The Earth stops spinning.

All three deaths have been ruled homicides. Autopsies performed on Karla Goodrow, Mary Wilkins, and Bernice Valgood reveal that all three victims were bound with rope before they were strangled.

Phelps' resident director rounds up all the girls on a weekly basis and stresses the importance of staying alert. Notices are posted all over campus.

Travel in groups.

Don't hitchhike.

Helen curses at herself.

Think rationally.

They have been on countless dates. She's even become familiar with his apartment in Ann Arbor. Harold is not a stranger.

Harold is not the Eastern Ripper.

With the back of her heel, she forces the rope and the rag beneath her seat. Harold hops in and turns the Oldsmobile away from Phelps hall. As he pulls out of the parking lot, she glances down to see one end of the rope still sticking out.

Helen bends forward to adjust her shoe and brushes the rope under the seat with the rest of her uncertainty. She takes Harold's hand in hers and listens as he talks about the restaurant they're going to.

"They have a *sauce au vert* that I could just fill a swimming pool with," he raves.

And indeed, the *sauce au vert* is lovely with her braised quail, and Harold reaches across the table every once in a while and runs his thumb over her knuckles. A swarm of claustrophobic butterflies invade her insides her face aches from grinning. Tingling warmth radiates from her heart to every inch of her body, even the skin behind her ears.

Helen drinks enough wine to feel heady and light, but not so much that she'll forget their perfect evening. Harold doesn't take a sip.

"You're worthy of a safe ride home," he tells her, squeezing a lemon into his ice water.

He escorts her to the car after dinner, nodding at the valet who brings the Oldsmobile around front. Harold tells the valet a joke about how much wine Helen has had and everyone giggles, including Helen.

Helen kicks off her heels and sits cross-legged in the middle of the front seat, scooting in close to Harold with her head on his shoulder as he drives, grateful that Harold keeps the center console tilted up and out of the way.

"You'll have to walk me to my door. The Eastern Ripper might be prowling campus tonight." She can't figure out why she says it.

The pause is too long. The air is suddenly coagulated and burning, the wine sour in her stomach.

Finally, "I feel nervous every time I drop you off on campus. But I don't think you have anything to worry about, Helen."

"Why shouldn't I worry?"

He pulls up to Phelps, shifts the car into park and inclines his head at her, his gaze thick with something she can't discern.

"A friend at the Ypsilanti Police Department says they're getting close," Harold explains. "Hopefully they'll have him caught before you return from Thanksgiving break. And then I'll be able to relax."

It's just past 11:00, well beyond curfew, but Helen lets Harold kiss her on the front stoop of Phelps anyway. The drawn-out goodbye finally ends when Helen slips into the front atrium, where she almost colides Laurie Sue Bradford, a sophomore from one floor up. Laurie Sue is carrying a stack of boxes, and Harold rushes in to catch one just as it topples out of her grasp She thanks him.

"Can I carry them somewhere for you?"

"My car is just out front," Laurie Sue grins, letting Harold take the rest of the stack from her. She bounds forward to hold the door open for him and waves goodbye to Helen. Before crossing the threshold, Harold turns and winks at her, and she feels like she's floating.

She leaves him behind for Thanksgiving break later that week. Harold calls her every other night, giving her just enough space to enjoy her family and still miss him. He ships a book wrapped in newspaper to her house. It's a Ray Bradbury novel she has to hide from her mother.

She loves it.

Her last night at home, she listens to the radio with her father before bed, dozing off on the couch until a rather panicked-sounding anchor jolts her awake.

The fourth victim of EMU's Ripper, found just last Monday, has just been identified as 21-year-old Laurie Sue Bradford. Laurie Sue was last seen leaving her dormitory around 11:00 Sunday night with a man matching the Ripper's description.

Her shoulders stiffen and her jaw clenches. Her whole body is tense and awake, panic working it's way out of her marrow. Helen walks in a fear-striken haze to her bedroom, the panic building with each step she takes.

11:00 Sunday night

In the living room, the anchor is still talking about Laurie Sue. Helen's eyes are watering, her chest is tight.

Investigators say they may be closing in on a suspect, but need more witnesses. If you have any information...

Her hand hovers over the phone. After countless RA safety meetings, Helen has the number for Campus Police committed to memory. She isn't quite sure what to do with it.

The phone rings before she can decide. She picks up the receiver and puts it to her ear, unable to manage words. She knows who is on the other end before he speaks.

"Helen?"

... authorities urge you to come forward.

"Harold." Her voice is barely a croak.

"Helen," he says, pure relief audible even from a hundred miles away. "I just wanted to call and... I wanted to tell you again how much I enjoyed taking you out the other night."

Sunday night, Helen recalls. She won't speak, not until she's sure every thought in her head won't come spilling out. Not until she can separate reality from irrational anxiety.

She hasn't scared him off. She isn't too much for him.

Harold? A killer?

Laurie Sue, her gratitude as she passed the boxes to Harold, her smile as she waved *goodbye* and held the door open for him.

"Did you hear?" The words fall from her lips. "Oh it's awful, Harold. Laurie Sue was killed by the Ripper. The same night you helped her carry those boxes."

Harold's nervous contemplation cuts through the prolonged silence.

Helen sinks to the floor, leaning against her bed with her knees pulled to her chest, gently rocking back and forth and biting her fingernails as she waits for him to say something.

"Well, doll," a deep sigh, "I did hear. In fact, I just got back from the police station."

Helen is very careful not to say anything. "I wonder..." He clears his throat. "Do you recall what time we got back to your dorm that night? It was awfully late, wasn't it?"

Helen nods, though she's not sure why. "Sunday night," she recalls, this time aloud.

Harold says nothing.

Harold? A killer?

"It was awfully late. I was glad to have you to escort me to the door."

"What time would you say I did that, Helen?" An icy edge, however slight, slithers into his voice. Helen keeps biting her nails. "Couldn't have been earlier than midnight, right?"

She waits to feel some primal intuition in the pit of her stomach; for her spirit guides or God or Laurie Sue to tell her what to do.

The radio is still ranting in the living room. She can barely hear it over the beating of her heart and the sound of Harold waiting for her to say something. The latter is the loudest. Deafening.

Again, law enforcement continues to urge anyone with information to call...

Harold loves her.

Harold. A killer.

Eleven, she wants to scream.

"Midnight or later if I have to guess, but I had so much to drink," she hears herself say.

She remembers the joke with the valet, the laughing. She almost vomits.

"Exactly. Anyway, the police might need you to make a statement about the time I dropped you off. They're just covering their bases." She can picture him waving it away; a nonissue, like a bothersome gnat.

"Of course."

"No need to fret about it. Anyway, sleep tight, doll. I'll see you the day after next."

Harold hangs up without waiting for her response. Helen listens to the dial tone until it cuts out. The receiver is still pressed to her ear as she looks down at the dial. The digits won't stop arranging themselves into the phone number she has memorized.

The voice on the other end sounds tired.

"Eastern Michigan University Campus Police, may I help you?"

About the Author

Abbie Pedrotte lives in Saginaw, MI, with her husband and pets. Abbie works for the READ Association and writes for *The Michigan Banner* and *Saginaw Township Living*. She attends Delta College and will graduate in spring 2025. If she isn't working, she's writing, and if she isn't writing, she's reading, running, hiking, lifting weights or baking.

Adult Readers' Choice Winner

A Place at the Table
Alexander Davidson

WINTER, 1926

I was born for the stage, but life had other plans. At my lower east side high school, where our long-in-the-tooth director had a hard-on for Shakespeare, I could strut the boards as Hamlet, Romeo, or Julius Caesar. Back home in Detroit's nascent Little Italy, I was merely Louie Russo, nephew of Alessandro De Luca, my mother's brother and owner of Gratiot Avenue's finest restaurant Bello Italiano. While the Motor City was thriving on immigrants crossing the Atlantic to help mass produce automobiles for Henry Ford, I dreamed of heading to Pittsburgh where Carnegie Mellon had established the first degree-granting drama institution in the United States. As I said, though, life had other plans.

When my father died, my mother and I couldn't cover rent for our apartment, and I learned that restauranteur was not the only item on my uncle's resume. He started offering me odd jobs, mostly running errands and passing notes. As I got older, Alessandro didn't see my passion for theater as a useless distraction like most; he saw an opportunity and a chance for me to contribute to the family.

INTERVIEW TRANSCRIPT DECEMBER 12, 1926
OFFICER DUNCAN O'MALLEY REPORTING
WITNESS: ETHEL ROSENBAUM

O'MALLEY: Ms. Rosenbaum, you didn't see anyone attack the victim, Samuel Ackermann?

ROSENBAUM: Officer, it's like I said. A garbage truck came out of nowhere sliding down these icy roads. The city really should be doing more to keep these streets safe in wintertime. I was just saying so to my neighbor, Barbara--

O'MALLEY: Ma'am...

ROSENBAUM: Right! The truck barreled around the corner and SLAM ran him right over. Flatter than a matzah. The driver must've had someplace important to be because he just kept going.

O'MALLEY: Were there any defining features of this truck?
ROSENBAUM: Oh, I really can't say. I'm not sure.
O'MALLEY: Anything would be helpful, Ms. Rosenbaum.
ROSENBAUM: There might've been a four-leaf clover on the logo?

I shuffled three blocks in Ethel's uncomfortable saddle shoes before disposing of the entire wardrobe – wig, prosthetics, cardigan, and all – in an alley dumpster. As part of my routine, I said a little prayer for the passing of Ethel Rosenbaum from this world. I enjoyed creating new characters and taking on their identities, but even as I hopped from precinct to precinct, it was better that I never played the same false witness twice. No matter how much I loved playing Carl, the alcoholic watchmaker, or Stewart, the football-loving mechanic, I had to lay them all to rest as soon as their testimony was complete.

Returning to Bello Italiano, I was welcomed by a gruff chorus of greetings from the men gathered around the restaurant and eating nothing. How I never understood growing up that we were actually a crime family is beyond me. Granted, the De Lucas were a much smaller organization focusing primarily on the running of alcohol as opposed to city-wide domination through terror and violence, but we held our own against the other Italian, Irish, and Jewish families fighting for a piece of the same pie.

I weaved through a room of congratulatory back pats and handshakes on my way to Alessandro's corner booth in the back. He sank into the smooth red leather seats while reading today's Detroit News. "So?" he said without looking up. Congratulations were not my uncle's thing. Why congratulate you for something he told you to do and expected to be done?

"Finished," I replied.

"News?" he asked.

Alessandro's second, Giacomo, slid out from a neighboring booth. "It was a risk to hit Sammy in Paradise Valley, boss, but no one seems to be looking our way."

"He shouldn't have double-crossed us by extorting our local businesses for bogus protection money. Let the Purple Gang go to Black Bottom for that," Alessandro said.

"Genius move, kid," Giacomo commented. "Sending the heat over to the Mulligans will distract those Jews and keep tonight's shipment of Canadian whiskey across the river raid free."

Alessandro folded up his paper as a new cook brought out a steaming plate of osso buco and placed it in front of my uncle. "My favorite, Anthony," Alessandro said, cutting into his veal. I caught the new guy's eyes for the briefest moment, the brightest blue.

"Pretty soon, your nephew is going to be running this neighborhood," Giacomo said.

Alessandro grunted.

I felt my stomach flip. Was it because of the compliment or Anthony's smile in my direction?

SPRING, 1927

Bello Italiano grew silent as my uncle walked in from the kitchen and took his place at the corner booth. Tensions were high since March's massacre between the Licavoli Squad and the Purple Gang in an apartment building downtown. The residual heat caused some ripples.

"Thanks again," Giacomo whispered.

"All part of the job," I replied.

INTERVIEW TRANSCRIPT MARCH 26, 1927
SERGEANT JOHN DONOVAN REPORTING
WITNESS: DYLAN MATTHEWS

DONOVAN: And that's when you heard the gunfire?

MATTHEWS: The machine gun was so loud! Just constant blasting through the building.

DONOVAN: And you think you can identify the men from the shooting?

MATTHEWS: How much longer will this take? My grandmother gets worried if I'm away too long. She has dementia, and I need to be there to take care of her.

DONOVAN: We'll get you out of here in a jiffy, son. I just need to show you a lineup and see if you can identify the shooters.

MATTHEWS: Happy to help, Officer.

One of the six men, of course, was Giacomo. No one was ever convicted of those murders, in part thanks to the meek and nerdy but gentle-hearted Dylan Matthews I created. Why waste time and money bribing and terrorizing witnesses when you can just invent them like the De Luca family does? It hurt to put that character to rest, mostly because Anthony said the horn-rimmed glasses made me look sexy. Maybe I'll see about buying another pair as a gift to myself. I stared at the porthole of the swinging door that held Anthony behind it. I imagined our next rendezvous in the pantry.

Giacomo nudged me from my daydreaming, and I refocused.

When Alessandro had taken his seat, we filed into our usual places around him. Only Giacomo joined him in the booth. I both did and didn't long for a spot at that table. It meant being included and having a place of power, but as I told my mother on a regular basis, I was not in this life for the long haul. This was a means to an end. I would save enough to get out of Detroit and head to Pittsburgh. I wasn't a real criminal; I was just playing one.

All heads in the room turned to stare at the boy who was the main event. He was a few years younger than me with tanned skin. He nervously fumbled with a cap in his hands. Alessandro nodded for him to proceed.

"They've struck a deal, you see," the boy started. "I overheard them on the back nine."

This was one of the informants from the Detroit Golf Club. Arrogant men of power typically ignore those beneath them in plain sight.

"It's a bridge," the caddie explained. "They plan to break ground in August. It will cross the river into Canada. Mayor Smith promises to beef up border security but assured Abe Bernstein that he could still get his alcohol through."

"The Purple Gang is using City Hall to remove the competition," Giacomo deduced. "Once that Ambassador Bridge is up and running, it'll be helluva lot harder to run liquor across the river."

"You can go, Mikey," Alessandro told the caddie. "Rest assured that your father's operation will be looked after."

"Thank you, sir," the caddie mumbled. He bolted for the door.

"We have to stop that bridge," Alessandro decided. "We'll do what we have to do."

"I'll get some men brainstorming," Giacomo suggested.

While the rest of the gang started planning, I slunk into the kitchen where Anthony was chopping asparagus for tonight's risotto. My heart somersaults every time Anthony looks up from his counter and smiles to discover me. That smile and those damn blue eyes.

Our hands found their natural places as our bodies pressed against each other in the pantry. Our hunger for each other was great, but Anthony still managed to stumble across some words and phrases in between kisses.

"I'm just... worried... about you," he said.

"Don't be."

"But it seems... to be getting... worse."

I pulled back. "What do you mean?"

"I know you see it, too, Louie. It's not just the thefts and the murders. It's the family itself. The De Lucas are starting to turn on their own neighborhood. Gus at the dry cleaners had to pay $1,000 last month for protection. When he asked what would happen if he didn't pay, Alessandro threatened to burn down the shop. It was one thing when your uncle was carving out a place for our community to be safe, but now he's only in it for himself."

What was I supposed to say to this? I hadn't known about these changes, but what would I have done if I did? I was so wrapped up in myself, that I barely noticed those around me. Anthony had noticed, though. Anthony had cared. Anthony was a better person than I. It made me want him even more. Dare I say, love? Was I falling in *love* with Anthony?

Lost for words, I pressed my lips to his, and Anthony reciprocated.

Suddenly, the pantry door crashed open as Alessandro came barreling through.

"Anthony, do you have any more of those cannoli from last—"

Anthony and I shoved ourselves away from each other so forcefully that we crashed into the shelves, knocking fettucine to the floor.

Alessandro's face went from white to red to purple in a matter of seconds.

"What the f--- is going on here?!"

SUMMER, 1927

After that day, Anthony never returned to Bello Italiano. I didn't hear from him again. Two weeks later, I read in the paper that he was engaged to a nice Catholic girl. I said my own little prayer, this time mourning the death of what could have been and scolding myself for thinking that it ever could be.

I lost myself in my work, and there was a lot of it. As the groundbreaking date for bridge construction grew closer and closer, the De Lucas got more and more desperate.

INTERVIEW TRANSCRIPT JUNE 10, 1927
OFFICER DANIEL FLANNERY REPORTING
WITNESS: GORDON ROCCO

ROCCO: Both of the armed robbers had tattoos all over their arms. One was completely bald with a glass eye. The other had hair that was almost orange and a scar across his neck.

INTERVIEW TRANSCRIPT JULY 23, 1927
OFFICER BRENDAN NEARY REPORTING
WITNESS: SHIRLEY SYLVESTER

SYLVESTER: But, Officer, he couldn't have set those fires because he was with me all night!

**INTERVIEW TRANSCRIPT AUGUST 1, 1927
CAPTAIN SEAN BUTLER REPORTING
WITNESS: LORENZO FERARRI**

FERRARI: There's no way the kidnappers were Italian. An Italian wouldn't be caught dead in those British suits.

Anxieties were high after last night's job went south. The De Lucas organized a series of raids on construction companies, figuring that missing supplies would delay the inevitable. However, one location ended up having a police guard. Things got crazy, and two of Detroit's finest were gunned down. The family didn't need this kind of attention coming to their door.

"Louie will send them in the opposite direction," Giacomo said.

Alessandro said nothing. He hadn't talked to me, let alone looked at me, since that day in the pantry. He hadn't told anyone either.

"Louie's the man!" Giacomo had taken it upon himself to be the morale-booster, which apparently meant drinking and serving booze. "The De Lucas aren't going down for this. We're here to stay!"

The drunken mobsters cheered.

"Even after you're gone, Alessandro, we're in good hands with Louie."

"Shut up," Alessandro growled.

"What?"

"Shut the hell up!" Purple-faced, Alessandro exploded, "I'm not leaving my legacy to a degenerate like him!"

"Alessandro..."

"I didn't build our reputation from the ground up just to hand it over to a filthy homosexual!"

You could hear a pin drop. Everyone around me took a step back. I had worked to keep this part of myself hidden in order to be accepted by this group that had become my family. That was all over now. I needed them to understand that I was still me. I reached for Giacomo, pleading with him.

"Don't touch me, faggot!"

A knife to the heart. Giacomo's betrayal hurt more than Anthony's abandonment, more than Alessandro's betrayal. Then I remembered this avuncular man who helped raise me was also the man who plowed down the competition with garbage trucks.

Nothing needed to be said. At that moment lights flashed, sirens wailed, and a police raid on Bello Italiano cleared the room and brought everyone downtown.

INTERVIEW TRANSCRIPT AUGUST 9, 1927
CHIEF WILLIAM LEARY REPORTING
WITNESS: LOUIE RUSSO

LEARY: You're safe here. They can't see you through the glass.
RUSSO: I'm familiar with a police lineup, Chief.
LEARY: Don't I know it. You could spend the rest of your life in prison with the counts of perjury we have against you, kid.
RUSSO: I don't know what you're talking about.
LEARY: You've lived a life of dishonesty. I'm offering you a ticket out. Just tell us everything we need, and you can walk free. All you have to do is identify those involved. Can you do that?

Alessandro, Giacomo, and a handful of familiar men stood against a wall that measured their heights. All were guilty, but there was no way I was going to snitch on my family. I would just play the game as I always did. They turned their back on me, but I'd prove myself to them. Everyone'd be free in a few hours. Free to leave the precinct. Free to return to Bello Italiano. Free to return to our neighborhood. If I played this right, I could fix everything and be an accepted member of the group again. Everything would go back to normal.

Normal. I remembered Anthony's last words. His concern for the neighborhood under the thumb of Alessandro De Luca. His desire for something better for his community. Something that would not be possible under the current leadership.

I raised my hand and pointed.

SPRING, 1932

The kitchen of Bello Italiano bustled with cooks all preparing the classic menu items that lower east side Detroit had come to love and appreciate. I pushed past the swinging door and made the rounds to crowded tables of loyal customers and happy neighborhood families. While my dream was to tread the stage, I found this type of spotlight suited me just as well. I had found the role that I was meant to play, one of a positive community leader.

I took my place at the corner table. The red leather booth had never felt better.

About the Author

Alexander Davidson is an author, secondary educator and donut aficionado. As seen on CBS Detroit and Buzzfeed Books, Davidson has a passion for literacy and creating lifelong readers, one student at a time. He has presented at multiple teaching conferences at the local, state, national and international level. His debut novel, *The Visitor's Choice: A Search to Make Things Right* (Ferne Press), received multiple accolades from the Mom's Choice Awards and the Purple Dragonfly Book Awards. He is the reader and writer behind @MrD_Reads on Instagram, where you are sure to find your next great book recommendation. If he is not reading, writing or teaching, this travel enthusiast might just be planning and dreaming about his next global adventure.

Adult Published Finalist

Forty Autumns
Edward Burkhead

It was autumn again. Of course it was autumn. It felt like it had always been autumn for them. In memory, their love hadn't felt like a continuous thing, but rather like it had existed as a series of discrete Septembers, one clicking against the next like the beads of an abacus.

This was their season. The time just past the equinox, when the shadows of trees stretched long like black taffy, and the leaves would crinkle brown and gold and red. When the sun would hide behind the dark maples, shy and cold, painting hazy watercolors across the sky.

Forty autumns ago they'd had their first date. Their first kiss had happened soon after. Thirtynine autumns ago they'd had their first real fight. Twenty-eight autumns ago they'd gotten married.

They had wandered forty autumns of woodland trails, watching squirrels stuff their cheeks fat with walnuts. They'd eaten forty autumns of candy and cider and sugar-crusted donuts. As he navigated his car into the parking lot, it made a cruel kind of sense that it would be autumn now too. Autumn at the beginning. Autumn at the end.

The car he parked now, in the fortieth autumn, was much nicer than the one he'd driven that very first autumn. It was black and fastidiously clean. There was no rancid scent of old hamburger wrappers, no duffel bag full of old laundry. Rust and stains and dusty dashboards had surrendered to a lavender-scented tree that hung from the rearview and regular trips to the car detailer.

The man was the same. He looked different, after forty autumns. His once-blonde hair was now like pulled-apart cotton. Old man lines marched across his face. His twice-broken nose was chiseled and beveled and jagged at the edges. But the man was the same. The same steady green eyes. The same crooked, impish smile. The same soft, steady voice that always sounded a little sad.

He stepped out of his comfortable car. He stood on the concrete sidewalk. He mapped out the path to the clinic's entrance with his eyes, counting and planning and measuring the steps to the door. It was a beautiful autumn day. Just barely warm. The clinic was nestled in the woods, surrounded by trees that had turned rich gold. A sussurus came. The trees trembled in the autumn breeze. A forlorn sigh. Dead and dying leaves scattered across the pavement, sounding like pebbles passing through a rain stick. He trembled and squeezed his eyes shut. The sound reminded him too much of sand in an hourglass. Time was passing. Leaving him behind. Moments were trickling by. Seconds were being lost.

The maple leaves danced on the wind, pointing the way to the clinic's door. Beckoning him forward like a thousand gold-clad butlers. Come in, the butlers seemed to say. Be our guest. You are welcome here.

He didn't want to enter the clinic. He didn't want to be welcome. His feet carried him to the doors anyway. He found himself in a small circular room. There was no one to greet him, no smiling doctor or nurse to give advice like there had been in the days that had led to this one. Such things didn't matter now. What could they say? What advice could they give at this juncture? The decision had been made. Words were pointless.

A small black book rested forebodingly on a wooden lectern. A black felt pen had been tethered to its spine by a miniature noose. He took the book in his hands, touching the soft leather of its cover. It was filled with messages of love, and stories, and photographs, and even a cartoon doodle of a man and a woman holding hands while a cat slept before a fireplace.

The messages followed a theme. We'll miss you. You'll be missed. I will always remember waking up on Christmas morning and decorating sugar cookies with you. Words can't say what you mean to me. Love you. Miss you.

The man's throat felt tight and hot. Like he was choking on a hot coal. He uncapped the pen, held it above the last blank page in the book. His hand shook. He recapped the pen without writing anything. He went back outside. He collected a maple leaf. Not a gold one. Most were gold but he didn't want a gold one. He picked up the reddest, crunchiest maple leaf he could find. It looked like it was blushing. Back inside. He collected the leaf and the book in one hand. He pushed his way through a door on the left.

This room was also a circle. The second of three. He tried not to think of the circles of hell, but failed. He knew what was happening today. He didn't consider it a sin himself, but what if he was wrong? What if hell was real? What if a judgmental God was going to send her there?

Or maybe he was there himself. Maybe hell wasn't a lake of fire, but a beautiful autumn day. The last beautiful autumn day.

He followed the curve of the wall. It swept from left to right like the spiral of a nautilus shell. The room was white and comfortable. Huge windows looked out into the woods. There was a white couch raised from the tile floor on chrome legs. There was a white kitchenette along the curving wall, and then a door he didn't want to look at, and then a door that led to the bathroom, and a door that led outside.

In the center of the circle, sitting in her wheelchair like it was a throne, was her. Her eyes were closed. She was asleep. Her skin slumped heavily on her skeleton like a deflated balloon. It was marked with scabs and scars and other signs of her condition. A cannula in her nose connected her to a large white oxygen tank.

He stood in front of her, listening to the ocean wave sound of her breathing. Watching her sunken chest rise and fall like a listing ship. Something enormous and heavy came over him. An emotion that was too large and too plural and too painful to name. It was like an animal trapped inside of him, trying to gnaw its way out through his chest. It was like a kidney stone of the soul. The feeling was too big for him. Too big for any mortal heart. It stretched him, bloated him, as if he were a python swallowing an animal that was too large to digest. He opened his mouth. Tried to say her name. Failed. Tried again, and gave up when the only sound that came out was a whimper.

He touched her cheek softly with the back of a knuckle, as if he were wiping away a tear. He smiled as her as she opened her eyes. She smiled back.

"Hello."

"Hello."

He handed her the leaf. She reached up to take it. Her hands shook. Her forehead wrinkled and strained from the effort. Even that small movement was enough to overexert her. Her too-thin fingers trembled rebelliously, and fell short, grasping at air. With slow and careful motions, he caught her fluttering hands and closed them around the leaf.

She smiled again. A big smile. It spread across her face like ripples on a pond. "You. Brought. You brought. Me. A leaf."

"You always said autumn leaves were prettier than spring flowers."

"It. It's. It's. Crunchy."

"Of course it is. The crunchiest I could find."

"My. Favorite. I. I. Love it. That's. That. That. Is so nice."

His heart pounded. Her body was betraying her, but he was glad that she was still capable of being happy. Of expressing joy in little things. Her facial muscles were slack and atrophied, but the joy in her eyes was the same joy he'd seen for forty autumns. He loved the way she felt joy with her whole heart. He was a cynical creature. Guarded. Happiness made him suspicious. But not her. She enjoyed life without hesitation and without fear.

"You should save your breath."

"What. For."

She was still smiling, but it was like a shadow had fallen between them. A cloud drifting in front of the sun. She was right of course. What was the point in trying to save her breath now? It was a silly thing to say. But his instincts to take care of her, to keep her safe, were well-worn. A forty autumn habit. It felt wrong, deeply, impossibly wrong, to ignore them now.

They stood for a few minutes without speaking. She looked through the tall panes of glass and watched as bronze maple seeds helicoptered down to the soft dirt. A red cardinal hopped through fallen leaves, searching for grubs and worms. It twitched its triangle head in furious desperation as it tried to find an answer to its hunger.

He wanted to say something to her. Anything at all. Something profound to let her know what she meant to him, to summarize and eulogize the life they'd shared together. Something light-hearted to cheer her up, to make her laugh, to make facing the end a little easier. Over the years they'd shared a thousand inside jokes. Forty autumns of humor that only they understood, in their exclusive club for two. Now he couldn't think of a single one.

Her fingers fluttered up to find his. Her smile became a grin. It was a subtle difference. A minute change in the curvature of her lips. A shift in the cant of her eyes. But he could tell the difference. He had studied her smile for decades.

"You. You. Take. My breath. Away." She gave him a valiant but unsuccessful attempt at a wink. "G-get it?"

He smiled but stifled his laugh. He didn't trust himself to laugh. "I get it."

Of course she hadn't forgotten how to joke. Leave it to her to find a way to cheer him up. He was supposed to be the one comforting her, giving her courage and love, but she was the brave one. The strong one. He held her left hand with his left hand. With his right hand, he massaged her neck and shoulder blades. Drawing gentle circles. Careful not to press too hard.

There were still no words. He supposed there wasn't much left to say. Last week they'd had their final fight. He'd begged for to see another doctor, to keep trying, to not give up. At the very least to let the end come as a surprise. It was one thing to know that death would come, more probably sooner than later, but it felt so much different, so much worse, to watch her choose to willingly leave this world. To stand here and know that these were the very last moments. That it was now or never. That this was goodbye. That there would be no second chances. Forty autumns had come and gone. Only a small, pitiful, handful of minutes left.

How was he supposed to bear that? He knew he had been selfish. He knew she was hurting and that she'd made the decision because she wanted the ending to come on her terms. But he'd started that fight anyway, weak man that he was. She had stood firm. She was decisive like that. Always had been. She knew what she wanted. He knew if made those same arguments now, they would end the same way. He didn't want to spoil the last moments with a fight he'd already lost.

He showed her the black book. He showed her the photographs people had pasted into it. People who'd loved loved her. He showed her forty autumns. Forty summers. Forty springs. Forty winters. Apple orchards and unwrapped Christmas gifts and fireplaces that crackled. Painted murals and blown glass and decorated cookies and the cat lurking under the couch. He showed her camping trips on the beach in an olive-colored tent. Empty wine glasses. Weddings. Bicycle trips through the Italian countryside, the Alps visible in the distance. He showed her love.

"Did. Did. Did. You. Write. Anything?"

He froze. A cornered deer. His whole body burned with shame. He opened his mouth to try to explain, but no words came out. Her fingers found his again. Comforting him. Neither of them was capable of doing much speaking. She was out of breath, and his words had frozen inside of him. But after forty autumns of holding hands, they had developed their own special, coded language. A language of gentle pressures and interlaced fingers that said things clumsy words could not.

"Can. We. Walk?"

"Yes."

He wheeled her through the door that led outside. They walked together for the last time. They made their way down a path drowning in fallen yellow maple leaves. Two small and lonely sailors upon a golden sea. He made sure to run her wheelchair over the crunchiest leaves.

The breeze came again. The leaves tornadoed around her. She laughed.

"Thank. You."

"Of course." He hesitated. "Is there anything else you want to do?"

She gave him another effortful wink. It was a wink that used every one of the muscles in her face. "Oh. I. I. Have ideas. The bed is. Very big."

"The bed you say?"

"Yes. The. Bed."

"What would our parents think though? They would be scandalized if they caught us."

"Then. They. Better not. Catch us."

"It's worth the risk. How can I resist someone as beautiful as you?"

"You. Liar," she said. But she looked pleased.

They arrived back at the door. Back inside, there were three nurses in white uniforms. He didn't look at their faces. He hated them. He stared at their shoes.

He embraced his wife for the last time. Held her as tight as he dared. Even now he was afraid of bruising her. Her skin was so soft and papery. He held her as if he were an anchor, tethering her whole soul to the world. He knew he would have to let her go. He knew that this was the destiny of all people. To love. To be hurt. Heartbreak and abandonment could not be avoided. They were facts of life. The inevitable consequence of humans being temporary, mortal things. Everyone leaves, and everyone is left.

But this felt so personal. This was more than he could bear. How was he supposed to say goodbye? It was one thing to be swept apart by old age and disease and failing organs. It was another to walk away.

He released her. The nurses wheeled her away. They handed her the little black book and the red leaf, as if they were talismans for her journey.

They took her to the door that he couldn't look at.

"Wait," he said.

He took the book from her. He uncapped the felt pen. He turned to the only blank page in the book. The last page. He wrote the things he couldn't say: *I don't know how to do this. I don't know how to say goodbye. I don't know how I'm going to live without you. But I'll do my best to figure it out. I love you. Goodbye.*

He kissed her for the last time. They held hands for the last time. They touched one another's faces. They stared into one another's eyes for the last time. Green eyes reflecting blue. For the last time.

The moment passed. Another grain of sand gone in the hourglass. He stepped back. The nurses took her through the door of the last room. She turned and gave him a little wave. She blew him a kiss. He caught it and tucked it safely into his pocket.

And then she was gone.

This was how it had to be. He wasn't allowed in that room. He understood why. How could he just let her go? Forty autumns of keeping her safe. Loving and protecting and caring for her. And now he was just supposed to let her go and get hurt? Impossible.

He didn't know when it happened. There was no signal given when the love of his life died. The world didn't tremble. The seas didn't boil. The maples outside kept drifting in the wind. The red cardinal kept hunting for breakfast.

He hoped she didn't regret it. That she hadn't changed her mind at the last minute, and he hadn't been there to save her. He hoped she was at peace.

At some point one of the nurses handed him the book and the crunchy red leaf. He took them without looking up. He stood alone in the room for a long time.

He opened the book, looked through the memories again. He turned to the last page again to read the words he'd written. Anger filled him. The words seemed inadequate and incomplete. Why couldn't he have written something better? Why couldn't he have said what he wanted to say? Something that encompassed all the love of forty autumns. Now she was gone and he would never get the chance.

But his words weren't alone. In shaking, almost childlike letters, she'd written him something back.

Don't forget to feed the cat.

He smiled. A choking laugh came out of him.

He walked outside. It had turned a little chilly. The autumn leaves blew across the parking lot. He took the crunchy red leaf he'd given her, held it in his hand for a moment, and released it into the breeze.

About the Author

Edward Burkhead is an instructor in the Professional Trades Department at Jackson College where he teaches courses in mechanical design, robotics and industrial automation. He has also been writing fantasy and speculative fiction since 2019. His teaching is focused on helping people achieve excellence through consistent, deliberate practice. His writing focuses on exploring human experiences in fantastical realms.

Adult Published Finalist
Yellow Eyes in a New World
Max Bufkin

It had no name. It didn't need one in the time it had been born. Names were for people, and it wasn't considered a person even though it could eat, talk, and feel the way they did. For almost two hundred years, it had laid dormant, sleeping, waiting without a name. Then, one day, it awoke in a future that was unfamiliar to its yellow glass eyes. Someone had figured out a way to wake it from its dreamless slumber: a girl with bright pink hair.

"Welcome back," she had sung.

Her hair was pulled back into two long pigtails like the strings of a party streamer. A pair of faded hemp overalls were pulled on over her plump figure, the knees patched with fabrics of differing patterns. She was holding a large brass wrench, which she rested over her shoulder with a toothy grin.

The girl's pale brown skin glistened in the morning sunlight coming from the four arched windows in the room. Dangling, beaded plants hung from the gold ceiling and grew from pots on the bamboo floor. A machine filled with bubbling water sat in the corner, a vapor shooting from its spout like the tip of a whistling teapot. At the side of the room was a cozy-looking hammock filled with pillows and stuffed animals.

The nameless machine that the girl had awakened stared at her quizzically, still groggy from its two-hundred-year nap. It swiveled its head from side to side, its mechanical neck clicking with each slight turn. It was sitting on a cold metal workbench littered with tools and blueprints.

"Where–?" it began to ask.

"Longvine, Australia. But if you want specifics, we're in my house." the girl answered with a slight chuckle. "I found you half-buried in the rainforest while I was out foraging. You were in pretty rough shape but in good condition, considering how old you are. I repair old stuff all the time; it's kind of my job, so I thought I'd do the same for you."

"Who?" it asked, pointing to the girl.

"I'm Galah. And you are...?" she answered, holding out her hand.

"I have no name."

Its cold metal fingers wrapped around hers and shook.

"Well, that won't do! Everybody should have a name."

"I'm not an everybody."

"Well, you're a somebody."

It shook its head, then reached up and tapped the number printed on its chest. Galah took back its hand and slid it further down its chest to where its heart would have been if it had had one.

"That was a long time ago. Things are different now," she explained. "I won't give you a name unless you want one. I'll respect whatever you choose."

It had never been given a choice before, let alone the respect of a human being. The circuits in its head fired wildly, trying to process the words of the strange young woman who'd thrust it into the future.

"I would like a name," it said after a moment of silence.

"Hmm," Galah thought, tapping a finger to her chin. "Most of the people here are named after animals or plants, so how about...Plover? The metal on your body reminds me of a gray plover bird."

The two-hundred-year-old machine searched the word 'plover' in its head, pulling up an image of a fat white bird with black and brown markings.

"Yes, that will do," Plover said, blinking the image away. "I am grateful for the name, but...I don't understand. You treat me like one of your own–took the time to repair me–why?"

"Bots aren't treated the way they used to be a hundred years ago," Galah explained. "When bots were first made, we didn't know if you were alive in the same sense we are. But as time went on, people started to realize you had feelings, ones just as complex as our own. You felt fear, pain, sadness, and yet we were working you to the bone and treating you as less than human. It took a long time and a lot of work, but bots are considered people now–not just tools."

"C–Could you show me?" Plover asked.

Although its voice was artificial and crackled out of an old speaker, Galah could still hear its desperation. She nodded, taking its hand and helping it off the workbench. Plover's spring-jointed legs stepped onto the rough bamboo floor, creaking with each step.

"By the way, how should I refer to you?" Galah asked.

"What do you mean?"

"Are you a she, he, it, they–?"

"Just 'it' is fine," Plover said. "You get to choose such things in this new world?"

"Well, you know yourself better than anyone. It makes sense that you would get to choose who and what you are," Galah explained. "Oh! That reminds me; you probably don't know about true names, do you?"

Plover shook its head.

"Okay, so when someone is born, they're given what's called their 'first name.' But as they grow older and discover more about themselves, they get to choose their 'true names.' Some people choose to keep their first names their entire lives. But then there are people like me who find their first names don't suit them the older they get." Galah explained. "So, I guess I technically gave you your first name, but you can choose a true name whenever you feel ready."

The thought of such a choice overwhelmed Plover. It had never been allowed to choose anything, and now it was allowed to choose whatever it wanted. A strange sense of embarrassment washed over it, feeling ashamed for its lack of personality after centuries of conformity.

Galah, reading the anxiety on its face, gently tapped its shoulder.

"I know this must be a lot to take in, but I'll walk you through it, okay?" she said comfortingly. Plover nodded with a hint of hesitation.

It shielded its eyes as Galah pushed open the front door, embracing the afternoon sunlight. Together, they walked down the spiral staircase jutting out from the side of Galah's domed house. Similar hill-shaped houses rose all around them, built to fit into the landscape. The houses were taller than they were wide, accommodating generations of different families. Enormous trees with snake-like branches loomed around them, filled with colorful, fluttering birds. Solar panels glistened on the rooftops, and the gord-like lanterns hung from the trees.

"You rely on the sun for energy?" Plover asked curiously.

"Yes, and now you do, too," Galah said, pointing to the solar panel built into Plover's back. "You used to run on batteries, but now you don't have to worry about finding a pair to stay alive. Just sit in the sun a little each day, and you'll be good to go."

Plover awkwardly touched its back, feeling the smooth glass-like metal jutting out from between its shoulders. The solar panel was made of octagonal panels and arched away from its spine like a tortoise shell. If it closed its eyes and focused, Plover could feel the sunlight being absorbed through its back, warmth running through its circuits like blood through veins.

Galah and it walked over an ivy-covered bridge hovering over a raging river. She leaned over the wooden railing and pointed toward the beautiful blue-green water rushing below them. In one of the foamy rapids, a series of fan-like devices spun with the current. Bubble-shaped netting bulged out from the fan, keeping the fish from getting trapped inside.

"We don't *just* rely on solar power; we use water and wind as well,"

Galah explained.

Plover could see a wind farm off in the distance, sitting at the top of a green hill. The same bubble-like netting encircled the fans, letting the wind blow through while keeping the birds from harm's way.

"We fought against nature for a long time, but it wasn't a fight we were going to win. So, we had to learn to work with nature instead." Galah said.

"I always wished..." Plover began quietly, gripping the railing. "...I could be one with nature the way you are."

Galah looked at it for a moment, soaking in its words. Her amber eyes were soft yet heavy, the pupils laying on her bottom eyelid like the sun resting on the horizon.

"Well, we weren't always one with nature. To be honest, we still aren't. We've learned how to work together, but we're far from being in complete harmony." she said. "Sometimes, even we humans forget that, despite how advanced we may become, we're still made of nature.

We're stardust and carbon, just like everything else. And so are you. You're steel, copper, and glass; you're made of nature too."

Plover held out both of its hands and stared down at them with its pupil-less eyes. The knuckles were bent pieces of metal, like the base of a seesaw. Suddenly, every groove, dent, weld, and wire in its hand looked just as organic as everything else around it.

A spring breeze swept across the ground, carrying the sweet scent of eucalyptus and golden wattle. The river gurgled softly, a pair of turtles sunbathing on an overturned branch raised above the water. A pack of small children raced across the bridge, laughing and chasing each other with cattails.

For the first time in its life, Plover felt alive. It wasn't just a machine that happened to have a charge, but an individual, conscious being. The sensors in its fingertips weren't just to keep it from accidental harm or to better serve its human overlords–they were there to let it feel, to experience the world around it.

"I want to see more," it said.

Galah smiled.

"Then let's introduce you to everyone."

She led Plover into an open-air market nestled in a lush green clearing. People of all races were gathered together, making and selling beautiful wares. There were carpenters, jewelers, farmers–artisans of all fields trading from one another. And amongst the sea of colorful faces were bots just like Plover, but even they differed slightly from one to the next.

Some of them were patched with different types of metal, some wore clothes, others wore just jewelry, but most were adorned with some sort of plant or another. There were several bots with flower crowns and necklaces, but a few had built living terrariums into different parts of their body. Older-looking bots had moss and mushrooms growing from their heads. These bots were so unlike the uniform, carbon copies Plover had been used to. Suddenly, it felt ashamed at its lack of uniqueness.

"Would you like me to buy you anything?" Galah asked, catching its gaze. "My treat."

"N-No. You don't have to–" Plover stuttered.

"Come on," Galah chuckled.

She walked over to a stall selling shawls woven from the fibers of banana leaves. Plover watched as Galah handed the shop owner a small golden trinket shaped like a grasshopper. The shop owner wound the trinket up and watched as it hopped and flipped playfully across the stall counter.

"My daughter will love this," the shop owner squealed.

They smiled, shaking Galah's hand and handing her a sage-green shawl with white tassels. Galah turned and wrapped the shawl over Plover's shoulder, clipping it together with a leaf-shaped pin.

"There you go," she said.

Plover gently touched the fabric, catching itself in a mirror hanging off the stall.

"You don't pay with money?" it asked, turning back to Galah.

"No one does anymore," Galah answered. "We mostly just trade or do favors for each other."

"But how do you decide who gets what?"

"We all work hard to make sure everyone gets the amount of food and water they need. If someone gets sick, our healers will help them. Beyond that, it's up to the person to decide how much or how little they want to work," Galah explained. But everyone contributes to our community in one way or another. We all want to do our part."

"And you? What do you do to help?" Plover asked curiously.

"I repair whatever's broken, just like my mother did."

Just then, Galah's nose caught the scent of something delicious. She licked her lips and grabbed Plover's hand, leading it further down the market. They came across a stall run by a sturdy woman with braided black hair.

Skewers of roasted vegetables sizzled on the grill in front of her, filling the market with a heavenly aroma.

"Two, please," Galah said, handing the woman a metal clip.

Plover was surprised when the woman raised her right leg, and it looked exactly like its own. She took the metal clip and pushed it into a slot on her knee, wiggling her leg.

"Ah, much better," she sighed.

She handed Galah and Plover each a steaming skewer straight off of the grill.

"You know I don't *need* to eat, right?" Plover asked.

"I know," Galah said. "But no one needs to watch the sunrise, or make food taste good, or climb a tree. You do those things because they make you feel good–because they make you feel alive."

Plover took a bite of spiced pumpkin and chewed on it thoughtfully. Though its sense of taste was dull, it could still identify the flavor and textures in its mouth. It swallowed, feeling the food break down into energy as it hit its synthetic stomach. The corners of its metal mouth lifted into a smile.

"Come with me; I wanna show you something," Galah said, taking its hand.

They walked through a path carved through the rainforest until they came across a gurgling gray stream. A miniature waterfall fell into the stream, splashing softly. Reeds sprouted along the pebbled ridge, swaying gently in the wind.

Galah sat beside the stream and motioned for Plover to join her. They sat side by side in silence, quietly picking away at the skewers in their hands.

"Thank you for today…for everything," Plover said, facing Galah. "When I went to sleep all those years ago, I wasn't sure if I ever wanted to wake up. I was tired. All I did was move boxes. Even as the world started to crumble around me and my limbs strained, all I did was move boxes. Then, one day, I finally collapsed. My body wouldn't respond anymore. I fell asleep. But then I woke up here, and suddenly, the world I knew was gone."

"It's not all gone," Galah said. "We still have our history and our cultures–there are still the same plants and animals that were here before. Nothing has disappeared; it's just changed." She pulled her knees up to her chest and rested her head over them. "I'm glad that you feel thankful. I was worried about waking you…I wasn't sure if it was what you would have wanted."

"I like this new world. I'm just sad I had to sleep two hundred years to see it." Plover said.

"Plover…I may have told a half-lie." Galah sheepishly began. "I told you I repaired you because that's what I do; I fix things. But that wasn't the whole story. The truth is…my mother died a little over a month ago."

The camera lenses in Plover's eyes dilated with surprise.

"Ever since I've felt lost…aimless," Galah explained. "When I found you here, getting pelted by the rain, you looked just as lost as I did. You were all alone, left behind by the world. And, maybe it was selfish, but I thought that if I repaired you, then we'd both be a little less lonely."

"I am sorry for your loss," Plover said. "But it is like you said; nothing ever really disappears; it just changes. Your mother...she's not gone, not entirely. She lives on through the Earth...and through you."

A tear ran down the side of Galah's face and dripped from her chin down into the dirt.

"Thank you," she whispered.

Plover's gaze moved back to the stream, watching the water glide across the pebbled stones and sediment.

"...How long does it take someone to choose a true name?" it asked.

"As long as they need. Some people decide right away; others take decades. Some people choose a different name each year. It all depends on what feels right at the moment."

"I don't know who I am yet or who I want to be," Plover said. "But I want to learn. Will you help me?"

Galah put her arm over its shoulder and pulled it close.

"Of course."

About the Author

Max Bufkin is a Michigan-based writer who focuses on themes like LGBTQ+ matters, found family and optimism. They are currently seeking a degree in communications while working for their campus's newspaper. As a racially mixed transgender individual, they have always strived to create works that uplift oppressed voices and imagine liberated futures. In the summer of 2024, they self-published their dystopian novel, *After Epilogue*, on Amazon Kindle and plan to begin working on the sequel in the near future.

Adult Published Finalist

Blue Star Mother
Vicki Berger Paulissen

Detroit
May 25, 1942

Mother held my left hand in an iron tight grip, her hands as strong as a man's from years working as a masseuse in a bath house. Her fingers were thick with bulging knuckles that reminded me of the scars that form on a tree trunk when branches are lost.

We were standing outside on Detroit's Michigan Central Station platform. I feared my fingers would snap like a rabbit's leg caught in a trap, but I resisted the urge to yank my hand away. Angling my head slightly I peeked up at her. Face drawn tight, she stood stiff, chest out, chin level, her eyes unfocused but staring straight ahead, waiting for the metal beast that would carry my 21-year-old brother, Chip, away. I leaned forward to look past Mother to catch a glimpse of my brother Tommy. He was staring down at his worn, but polished shoes, his eyes screwed shut. Mother was holding his right hand in the same, white-knuckled grip that grasped my left hand. The three of us, locked together, created a floodgate. My hand was becoming numb, but I bit the inside of my cheek and held on to Mother as best I could, hoping to block the tears that threatened to pour out of both of us.

Chip, standing on Tommy's left side, was dressed in his spring jacket, khaki pants, and white shirt he'd worn every time we'd seen him off to the seminary in Indiana. Just as he'd done then, he held the leather satchel that Mother had given him three years earlier for his high school graduation. As he looked down the tracks, the satchel bounced against his leg.

But Chip wasn't headed to Indiana and no amount of wishing would change that. He was now a private in the U.S. Army and going to Florida for basic training.

It had been hard for me to accept the fact that the U.S. Army considered

Chip a man. My oldest brother Ches, twenty-one when I was born, tall with broad, muscular shoulders, and a scratchy beard, his voice deep and demanding, was my definition of a man. Chip was none of those things. I was tall for an eleven-year-old girl, an inch taller than Tommy, who was 18 months older. Chip, about three inches taller than me, wore glasses and could still wear Tommy's shirts. He boasted a few straggly hairs over his lip that he shaved occasionally.

Chip had enlisted while Uncle Syd, Auntie, and I were traveling home from Lake Worth, Florida, where we had spent the winter months. For the last three weeks, my family had been on pins and needles waiting to learn about Chip's orders. Worry about where he would be sent and what he would have to do seeped into the house like a black fog. Mother forbid any word be spoken about it. "We'll know when we know," she'd said.

I was setting the dining room table after school, when Chip burst in the front door, letter in hand, and announced he was ordered to report to Camp Blanding in Florida.

Florida! Not Germany, not Japan, but sunny, warm, safe Florida!

Mother had been preparing dinner and came into the dining room when she heard Chip.

"Oh, Lord," she said, clutching her middle. She melted onto a dining room chair. "It's happening. Jesus, Mary, and Joseph." She covered her face with her hands. "Oh, God," she moaned.

I stared at her in disbelief. Didn't she understand? Chip was going to Florida! Not to some foreign country!

"I know exactly where Camp Blanding is," I said, skipping around the table in relief. The skirt of my school uniform flounced up with each step. "We pass the signs for it on our way to Lake Worth. It's just south of the Georgia border on the Dixie Highway. You won't be able to see the ocean from there, and you better be careful of the shrub grasses, they'll cut your bare legs," I warned, my words tumbling out.

"Helen Jane, shush. You don't understand," Mother said, her voice hoarse. She rose and went into the kitchen.

I looked at her receding back, confused. I turned back to my brother, shaking my head.

"She just doesn't know, Chip. Florida is a great place," I said, brushing off her warning. "On our way to Lake Worth this fall, we'll stop and take you to the beach. You'll love it!" I was sure I could convince Pa, my affectionate nickname for my uncle, and Auntie to spend a day or two near him before we went the five hours further south to Lake Worth. I began to plan an entire itinerary for him.

"Sis—" Chip started, but I ignored him in my exuberance.

"I'll teach you how to find the best shells on the beach, how to spot jellyfish—the man o'wars are the worst—and of course, we'll swim in the ocean. I'm a very good swimmer," I bragged. A lightbulb went off and I snapped my fingers. "We'll take you to St. Augustine; it's not far from the Camp. We were there a few years ago and I adored those old buildings! It's the oldest city in the country," I said, on my second loop around the table.

"Sis—" Chip's voice rose, but he still couldn't break through my excitement.

"Maybe we could even take you down to Lake Worth for a weekend and introduce you to Min and her sisters. Min's my best friend, you know."

I was on a roll now, already planning a romance between him and Min's sister Cecilia. "Her sister's—"

"Sis! Calm down!" Chip said, on the edge of shouting. "Take a seat." He stepped in front of me and put his hands on my shoulders lowering me into the chair still warm from Mother.

"That all sounds great, " he said, with a gentle smile, sliding into the chair next to me.

"But don't get your hopes up, I might not be there when you come through."

"Well, why not? There's German submarines all around Florida. I'm sure that's why they're sending you there," I said.

The look in his eye was worrisome.

He glanced down the hall toward the kitchen where we could hear Mother getting dinner together. He tapped the top of the dining room table with his index finger. I searched my brain for reasons for him to stay in Florida.

"I'm not going to Florida to fight, Sis. Camp Blanding is a training camp," he said, his voice serious. "I'm going there to learn to be a soldier. Uncle Sam's my boss, now. After training I'll probably be sent overseas." "But why?" I asked. "What about the German subs?"

"Nothing I'd like better," he gave me a wan smile. "Swimming in the ocean in the morning, sinking subs in the afternoon, believe me, but the fighting is in Europe and the Pacific Ocean, so who knows where I'll be sent." He shrugged his shoulders.

A *soldier*. Flashes of the movie *Gone with the Wind* came to me: bloodied, starving men in uniforms, guns pointed at each other, dying in the mud, lying in a makeshift hospital screaming *"No! No! Don't cut!"* Oh God, not Chip!

"No, no, no!" I refused to accept his words. "Did you know," I said, starting to feel desperate, "we use black-out curtains at the house we rent, so the Germans can't see us at night? And—" I paused for dramatic effect, putting both hands on the table and leaning forward, "Pa read about a German sub sinking a big tanker off the shore of Jacksonville. That's not far from Camp Blanding. That's why Uncle Sam needs you there." I pounded on the table with childish certainty.

Chip shook his head. "Camp Blanding is a training camp, Sis," he repeated, his voice steady. "The letter says I can expect to be there for seven weeks and then I'll get the next set of orders." He opened the letter and laid it on the table to show me.

I pushed it aside.

My voice started to rise as panic set in. *"No!"* I stood, formulating a plan. "We could hide you. Auntie and Pa will let you stay with us in Lake Worth, I'm sure of it. There's plenty of space there." I looked feverishly at him.

He jumped up, knocking the chair down behind him.

"I'm no coward," my lanky, skinny brother said, jabbing the air with his finger at me so forcefully I jerked my head back, afraid he'd poke me in the eye. "Uncle Sam called, and I answered. Now, no more talk like that."

"Helen Jane, stop your nonsense." Mother's voice was harsh. She stood in the hallway, facing us, wiping her hands on her apron. "Your brother's made a choice and he's a soldier now. He'll go where he's told." She narrowed her eyes at him. They were filled with anger, fear, and pride.

She looked at me then as if she could no longer bear to see him. "Right now, I'm telling him to go get cleaned up for dinner and for you to finish setting the table." She turned on her heel and went back to the kitchen.

Her words cut me, and my vision blurred. I stared at Chip, the brother who'd defended me from her when I was little, comforted me when our brother Jimmy died, and amazed me with his incredible ideas. How could he be a soldier?

"Stop that," he said gently. "I think I'll be quite handsome in a uniform, don't you?" He tried to smile, then pulled me in for a long hug. "Don't worry about me Sis, I'm going to be okay," he said, his voice low and full.

"But how will we know?" I whispered, squeezing him, so afraid to lose him.

"Well, I'm going to write you, of course. You promise to write me back?"

"I promise," I said limply, wiping my tears on his shirt.

He smelled of oregano, basil, and tomatoes. He'd had a job as a waiter since he left the seminary and moved back home. It wasn't a job he liked, but he was trying to save enough money to go to college. He had dreams of becoming an engineer.

He released me. "Promise me you'll help Ma. She worries too much," he said, handing me his handkerchief.

I agreed. It had finally dawned on me *why* she worried.

I did my best to stand tall on the platform, trying to keep the floodgate closed. I could feel the pressure of the crowd at our backs. Chip was going to have lots of company on his way to Florida. Half the folks crowding the platform were fellows his age. At least outdoors, the air was more bearable. The sweat of hundreds of nervous twenty-year old men, mixed with the sulfurous odor of burning coal reminded me of the smell of Auntie's bath house on a hot summer day. Inside the station the smell of body odor had been a hundred times more intense than a late summer laundry day in our basement where piles of my four brothers' sweat-soaked clothes putrefied the air.

A young couple stood to my right, pressed so tightly together it was like they were two adjoining pieces of a jigsaw puzzle. Their heads were tilted, and their hats hid their faces, but I knew what they were doing. They reminded me of my brother Vin and his new wife, Eileen. It made me sad that Chip didn't have anyone to kiss like that.

Vin was waiting for us in his car. The parking lot at the station was so crowded, he had to drop us off at the front entrance. He and a round-bellied Eileen, Ches, Mimi, Auntie and Pa had come to our house for dinner the night before. Mother had taken the day off and cooked a feast. My brothers joked and laughed good naturedly, patted Chip on the back and said, "those Huns and Japs better watch out!"

"Do you suppose they'll make you into a pilot, Chip?" Tommy had asked. "Flying a plane would be sweet."

"Oh, dear God, not a pilot," Mother said. Her hand flew to her chest as if to calm her heart. "Please Chip, don't let them put you up in one of those flying tin cans."

"Sorry, Tommy," Chip said as he put a hand on Mother's shoulder. "Pretty sure that's not going to happen. I hear the Army won't train fellas like you and me with glasses to be pilots. Gotta have perfect vision to fly a bird."

"Huh," Tommy said, disappointed.

"Well, that makes sense," Mother said, visibly relieved.

After dinner, Chip, Ches, Vin, and Tommy played a few hot games of euchre. It was just as entertaining to watch them as to play. They threw the cards down so fast I couldn't keep track of what suit was trump.

Everyone hugged Chip before they left. It was the first time I had ever seen my brothers hug each other.

I wondered when we'd all be together again.

A light, spring breeze, whooshed under the covered platform, as if clearing the way for the train. It ruffled my hair and dress. Mother had insisted we wear our best clothes to see Chip off. I knew she wanted to create a lasting family portrait for him, so that if he was scared or in trouble, he could summon a vision of us and it would comfort him and bring him back to her, to us.

She and I were wearing the clothes we'd worn to Vin's wedding; she in a plum dress and I in the burgundy velvet dress and navy bowler hat Auntie had bought me. With my free right hand, I kept pulling the dress down below my knees—it had gotten a little short for me. Tommy had buckled to Mother's demand and worn a white shirt and tie with an old pair of dress pants. It was apparent that the other women on the platform—girlfriends, sisters, mothers—had the same idea. They reminded me of the fashionable crowd at the theater in Palm Beach where Auntie, Aunt Anne and I had gone to see *Gone with the Wind.* I pushed that memory quickly out of my mind.

There was a slight vibration in the soles of my Mary Janes and a moment later, I heard the faint echo of a train whistle. A black dot appeared down the tracks to my left and raced toward us, growing larger and more frightening, until the platform vibrated with a deep rumbling and streaks of orange and yellow screeched past. The striped, silver sides of a locomotive spewing steam, came to a screaming halt five cars past us. There were only ten feet between us and the line of cars. When the train settled, Mother dropped my hand and Tommy's and raised hers as if shielding herself from the train.

The floodgate was broken.

Mother's hands shook, her fingers spread wide, as if pushing back an imaginary wall. Her face was scrunched in pain and tears spilled down. Chip dropped his bag and rushed to her side. She turned to him, then curled her fingers into fists and lowered them under her chin.

Chip gently enveloped Mother in a hug, whispering into her ear. After a few moments, she sniffed and smiled at him, nodding. She stepped back, swiped at the tears on her cheeks and took a big breath, in and out. Through the train windows, I saw passengers step down from the cars on the other side. Conductors stepped out on our side to usher travelers in. The crowd behind us started to push forward. I stepped back so I wouldn't be carried along.

Tommy picked up Chip's bag and handed it to him.

"You're the man in the house now, Tommy. I'm counting on you to take care of Ma and Sis," Chip said to him.

"I'll…I'll do my best, Chip," Tommy said. He put his hand up in a salute.

Chip stepped back to return it, then pulled him in for a long hug. Beneath his glasses, I saw tears well up in Tommy's eyes.

When Chip turned to me, I tried hard to smile, wanting to look pretty for him, but my heart was breaking, and tears had begun to fall. He pulled me into a big bear hug and whispered, "Remember your promises, Sis." I nodded. I tried to breathe him in, but all I smelled was burning coal. Then he was gone in the crowd of young men clambering onto the train, answering Uncle Sam's call. My heart pounded with the fear that we might never see him again.

Mother put her arms around Tommy and me and pulled us tight. Without a word, we looked for Chip through the windows. Within minutes, the train spewed and spit and started to move, gaining speed rapidly. We caught sight of Chip, waving from a window just as the line of cars whooshed past us. Suddenly, the space in front of us was empty.

We were standing on the platform, silent, and unmoving when an elderly woman approached.

"Was that your first, dear?" she asked Mother, her voice gentle and kind. Mother nodded silently.

"Take this home and put it in your window," she said. She handed Mother a red and white banner with a blue star on it, like the ones we'd already seen displayed in some of our neighbors' windows.

"You're a Blue-Star Mother now. We must stick together and support one another. Here's one of our pamphlets."

Later that night, Mother hung the banner in our front window. A lone blue star sat in the center, with plenty of space around it.

About the Author

Vicki Berger Paulissen, Ph.D., is a lifelong Michigan resident. She is researching the history of her hometown, Mount Clemens, and its connection to her family while writing a historical fiction novel based on its identity as Bath City USA. She enjoyed collaborating with her late mother whose memories fuel the story and who continues to act as editor-in-chief from beyond the grave. (She can hear her mother say the last sentence is too long!) Vicki retired in 2021 after 28 years of teaching Chemistry at Eastern Michigan University. She devotes her time to writing, being a member of the Chelsea Writers' Workshop and lives in Dexter with her husband of 35 years, Jerry.

Teen Judges' Choice Winner

Three-Legged Race
Sophia Constance Wegner

I touch the tips of my tennis shoes to the white line spray-painted on the grass. Today is sixth grade orientation, where I will see my new school and hopefully catch a glimpse of the next four years. Eighth and ninth graders are also here, to give us advice about junior high. I look across the soccer field to where they laugh and chat naturally with one another. They are so old. After today, I will be one of them.

It seems like we were hugging our teachers goodbye only yesterday, cheering as the bell rang, and waving from bus windows as we bid our elementary school farewell. A strange memory emerges as I think of my recent graduation. I run it over in my mind as I stare at the large brown building that will be my new school. When I walked out the door for the last time my teacher said quietly in my ear, "You are ready for this, Olivia. I know because you are brave."

Brave... the school is flat with staggered wings, a lot larger than my elementary school. The lowering sun kisses the rooftop, casting its beams across the slanted tiles. A shadow begins to form on the field. I will miss my old teachers, the playground, the library- I will.

But I did not cry on the last day of school like some of my classmates. During graduation all that consumed me was an eagerness about where I was going next. Now it is August, and school will start in only two weeks. I am ready. I am brave.

I scan the side of the grassy field that leads up to the parking lot. Sixth graders hop out of their parents' cars and I watch them drive away. When a girl with blonde pigtails exits a black SUV, I instantly recognize my best friend, Anne. From kindergarten up until third grade we would sit practically on top of each other during carpet time. Another girl with black braids hops out after Anne, and I realize she must be the girl who joined our class a few months ago. Her name is Marie and she is nice. As they walk onto the field I wave my hand high in the air. When they see me, Marie smiles and Anne waves back.

"Hey," they say simultaneously when they reach the white line. They both wear black leggings and cropped purple T shirts, which I would almost think were the same if Marie's didn't have a brand's logo written across the shoulder. It was almost like they planned it.

"Nice outfits," I say, and because it doesn't sound as pleasant as it did in my mind, I quickly change the subject. "Aren't you excited?"

Anne grins and nods at Marie "Eek yes! In the car, we were thinking of all the things we're gonna do once we're teenagers. Like drink coffee and wear makeup."

Wow. I was so caught up with junior high, I didn't even think about all the other parts of being a teenager.

"*And*," Marie adds, "having sleepovers."

They both giggle, and I wonder what's so funny about it. I want to ask, but something tells me I shouldn't; like I should understand why they're laughing. Instead, I pretend to laugh too. Then Marie asks Anne if she's seen the seventh episode of *Gauntlet of Desire*, a show I've never heard of.

Anne surprises me by saying she has seen it, and they start talking about characters and plot lines, their mouths moving faster than I can follow. I nod along as if I know exactly what they're talking about, until a man with a megaphone makes an announcement. I stifle a sigh of thankfulness.

"Welcome sixth graders!" His suit and tie tell me he must be our principal. "I'm sure you're all wondering why we're gathered on the soccer field today instead of the front of the building. Well, we decided that we want to have a little fun with you all before we start our tour... to kick off this year's orientation, we're going to hold the first ever Meadowbrook Olympics, starting with a three-legged race!"

Nervous giggles and gasps break out down the line of sixth graders and I grin. I did a three-legged race once at a family reunion. It was fun. The man describes the rules of the game and guidelines for the Olympics.

When he mentions the first game will have partners, I instinctively turn towards Anne. But she is facing in the wrong direction, looking at Marie. Something twists in my chest as I watch them make eye contact.

"You got all that?" The megaphone draws my attention back to the principal. "Go find your partners!"

I stare at the white line as I listen to the pact form between Anne and Marie, biting the inside of my lip. It's supposed to go without saying best friends choose each other first. Maybe she forgot. When Anne catches my eye she pauses her laughter. "Oh I guess you still need a partner. Maybe we could... um..."

I interrupt her. "That's no problem, I'll just find someone else!" I'm surprised at how unbothered I sound.

"Oh. Okay then...," she says, "well it's too bad we can't have groups of three."

Marie nods sympathetically.

That's fine, I convince myself, *there are plenty of nice people here.* I scan the crowd for whoever that might be. My eye latches onto a waving hand from a boy walking in my direction. I recognize Sam and feel relief. He's in ninth grade and lives in the house right across from mine. Our families have been friends since I was little, and we still get together with them at least once a month. We had a barbeque just this Sunday; I hadn't even thought to ask if he might be here.

"Hey Liv, do you need a partner?" He smiles as he reaches me. Liv is my nickname.

I nod that I do, and have to look up to see his face because he is a lot taller than me. Somehow, although I saw him only three days ago, he looks different. I stare at him curiously, trying to discover what it is. His clothes are blue jeans and a flannel shirt, nothing different from what he usually wears. I look at his face. The shadows that form under his cheeks and eyebrows make him look old. Has he always had blue eyes? He must've.

Finally I decide on the dark curls that barely fall onto his forehead. "Did you get a haircut?"

"No, not since Sunday! Why? Do I look different?" Sam laughs. Before I can respond he adds, "Hey nice shirt!"

I instinctively look down at my shirt, which is pink with a sparkly laughing emoji on the front. My cheeks warm. I know it was a compliment, but suddenly I wish I chose something else to wear today. Something more plain and stylish like Anne and Marie are wearing. I tell him "thank you" anyway.

Moving down the line, the principal hands a red bandana to a pair of girls. Soon, he will hand one to Sam and me. When we were younger, we would run into each other's backyards all the time. I had the playset, he had the trampoline- the best of both worlds. I still remember twirling on the swings, squealing as the metal chains unraveled. I remember the thrill of the trampoline, shrieking as we soared high and toppled down, landing on top of each other. I remember tackling him in a game of backyard football, and the night he taught me and my sister how to arm wrestle. I've given him hugs and high fives probably a hundred times before. But today, thinking about one of those red bandanas around our ankles makes me uneasy. I think about something else. Probably I'm just nervous about going into junior high. I'm sure the other kids are too... although I thought I was brave. Now, the man hands a bandana to Anne and Marie.

"How's Coco?" The question leaves my mouth before I realize it's on my mind. Coco is Sam's dog, and I have known her almost as long as I can remember.

"Good!" Sam shifts his weight onto his right foot. "A little naughty, though. Last night, she ate my dad's sock."

I giggle, even though it isn't that funny. Now the principal is headed in our direction, so I stare at the white line in front of my feet and wiggle my toes inside my shoes.

When he reaches us, he hands the bandana to Sam and they exchange nods. In a moment he has moved on to the next pair, and a nervous pit forms in my stomach. As Sam bends down to tie us together, I watch Anne and Marie do a handshake. Snap, clap, snap, clap... It is the same one I used to do with Anne. I feel Sam's skin press against mine right above our socks as he pulls the knot on our bandana. A chill rushes through me and I don't know why I'm suddenly afraid. I try to distract myself by looking around the soccer field and inspecting my new school. The sun is lower in the sky now and the shadow is longer... distorted and stretched over the soccer field, creeping toward the white line where we stand. A small outhouse, the only structure next to the field, makes me realize there is no playground. Not that there would be a playground at a junior high school... it just looks strange without it. Less friendly somehow, and more stern. The building is a lot larger than my elementary school, but long and flat, like a ball of cookie dough someone rolled out too thin. The windows are narrow too, all the way around. Inside them, it is dark. I think about my fifth grade teacher and almost wish she were here, before quickly changing my mind. I don't want her to know I'm not as brave as she thought. On the rooftop, sparrows sing songs back and forth. I wish I wore a different shirt.

Sam bends down slightly so he's eye level with me. "You ready Liv? We got this!"

I smile back in response, but can't hold his gaze for more than three seconds. What's wrong with me?

"Hey are you alright? You look a little pale." His blue eyes deepen with concern.

My heart skips a beat and I can't look at him again. *Are you alright?* It takes me a minute to process the question. "Uh yeah, just a little nervous.... about junior high." The last part comes out too quiet. Sam assures me it's normal to be nervous but that the school is great and I am going to love it. What he says is good. I just wished it made me feel better.

The megaphone crackles that the race is about to begin. On the sideline junior high students cheer us on. "On your mark..." Marie whispers something in Anne's ear. "Get set..." I swallow a butterfly back into my stomach. "Go!"

The teams yell and laugh as they stumble out onto the field. When Sam lifts his leg, he takes mine up with it. I can't help but notice that next to his, my legs look thin and my knees knobby. I try not to think about my stringy hair and childish clothes. My big toes press against my worn-out tennis shoes as we fumble forward, rubbing against the threadbare leather. I don't know when they got too small for my feet. The field is full of urgent voices, partners shouting instructions at each other, laughing, falling over. Sam and I don't give each other direction; we don't have to. We find our footing and develop an unspoken rhythm. Left, right, left, right. We make a good team. The setting sun forces me to squint as we advance down the field, until we cross into shadow, and it disappears in an instant. I notice every move Sam makes. Every breath he takes is loud and every twitch vibrates through me. My heartbeat alternates with the sound of our feet smacking the earth. *Pound, smack, pound, smack.* Left, right, left, right. *And maybe...* I'm afraid of more than just a new school.

Now, Anne and Marie are the only team close by, threatening to pass us on our right. They have their own rhythm, and they chant their steps in glowing unison. Something about their proud laughs and loud whispers make them seem older, although I could've sworn we were the same age a month ago. They are calm about our transition. Cool. Brave. They wear it well. *Why did I have to choose this shirt?* I glance back at Sam. His curls bob slightly as we move and his gaze is fixed on the ground in front of us, focused and strong. He is grown. I am not. Hot tears push against the back of my eyelids and clog up my throat, threatening to spill over. I don't let them. I'm not grown up yet, but I'm not a child either. Not anymore.

I push myself harder, forcing my stick legs to move quicker. Faster. Faster than Anne and Marie, who for some reason, I must beat. Sam adjusts to my speed and our rhythm picks up. I tune into the cheering coming from the teenagers on the sideline as Sam and I advance towards the finish. Sam says something to me which I can't make out, though his voice sounds encouraging. We are steps away now. For a moment, adrenaline rushes through me and I feel a thrill- the trampoline all over again. A breeze catches under my wings as we move closer. Left, right, left, right. I can hardly breathe. As our feet pound hard on the white line in unison, the exhilaration travels from the center of my body down my legs and into the ground with that one final step. Students cheer and Anne and Marie cross the line just steps behind us. Sam says something else I don't really hear as he unwraps the bandana that was holding us together. I look over my shoulder at the white line from where I started. It seems ages away, although I know it's only a few yards. The sun glints off the white giving it a soft glow, like a warm memory. I am in junior high now. Not old, not small. I will never go back to before that white line. A knot tightens inside me and the heat returns behind my eyelids. A crowd forms around us as other teams make it across the finish line and more junior highschoolers rush in to give high fives. Overwhelmed, I hear cheering and a whistle blowing. Teenagers are laughing in a sea of a hundred voices. I hear Bees are hum and sparrows sing. I see my school, the megaphone, the matching purple shirts. I see clovers swaying and the red bandana crumpled at my feet. And I see that white line... far away. I think about junior high and relay races, knobby knees and too-small shoes. I think about Anne with Marie, and Sam's blue, *blue eyes.*

Before I can realize why I can't hold my tears any longer, before I can worry about who might see me, who I'm supposed to be and who I'm not, I use the crowd to slip away toward the outhouse. The megaphone barks that the winners are about to be announced. I push free from the crowd and stare at passing grass, hoping no one will notice my red eyes. No one does. I tuck myself swiftly inside, into hot, sticky darkness. *You are ready...* the words burn in my chest, *because you are brave.* On the seat I bury my face in my knees, and hear my victory announced through muffled sobs.

About the Author

Sophia Constance Wegner is seventeen years old and is from Rochester Michigan. She has had a passion for creative writing ever since she was young. Any form of storytelling is fair game! She cherishes her three younger siblings, large extended family and savior Jesus Christ. She hopes to glorify Him and continue telling stories as she pursues animation in college.

Teen Judges' Choice Runner-Up

A Road to Travel
Zak Burns

Death came to Billings, Kansas, in a roaring crimson '68 Camaro, headlights cutting through the mist enshrouding the town in the hours before the sunrise could burn it away.

No one really noticed when he arrived, and no one really noticed when he left. No one died, and no one mourned. A few perceptions were shattered, but that really couldn't even be considered his fault, in the end.

He was just passing through of course, and after driving all night was really just looking for a good cup of coffee and a bite to eat.

He found what he was looking for, as so many do, at a diner a mile or two off of Route 66. The sun was just cresting over the highway when he pulled into the parking lot at Tony's Diner, a rectangular building situated next door to a run-down Super 8. The two were only divided by a shattered and weedy parking lot that currently held a tan station wagon with a crack in the driver's side window and, next to it, the Camaro, exhaust still softly puffing out of the tailpipe.

Katherine Deveraux watched the car pull in from the big bay window of Tony's, pulling her dirty blond curls up into a messy bun and hoping that her foundation hid the circles under her eyes.

"Doesn't look good to guests to see their waitress lookin' like that, dear," her boss, Tony himself, had told her. "Just try and look presentable, okay?"

Tony, in Katherine's opinion, rarely looked presentable. The years were weighing heavily on him, his back curving and his stomach bulging underneath the greasy apron that was his uniform. His lips were always shiny with spit, and his eyes had a filmy quality to them.

Tony had been an artist, once. He had done a mural on the walls inside of the diner, a recreation of Billings, an idealized version where the townsfolk were always smiling and the day was always bright and clear. That had been years ago, though, back when Katherine had been a girl coming into the diner with her momma and daddy on Friday nights for dinner, back when Tony's hands had nimbly held pencils and paintbrushes, back before they had snarled into the aching, bruised and scraped hands of a man who'd spent too long over the stoves and fryers that kept his business running.

The murals had long since faded into dull, erstwhile whispers of the past. Sometimes, though, on mornings like this one, when the sun rose in just the right way and Katherine was standing in just the right spot, for just a moment the diner would flood with a soft glow that gave those walls a new life and Katherine a new hope. For a moment she was a child again, when the day was always bright and her mother smiled, when this town had been her own little heaven.

The soft tinkling of the bell announced that the Camaro's owner had come in. He stood in the doorway for a moment, the morning light softening his angles and edges. Then he strode in, slumping onto one of the barstools in front of the counter.

Katherine leaned back onto the table behind her, plastering a smile onto her face. "What'll you be having, hon?"

The man leaned forward, almost as if to compensate for the space that Katherine had left between them. His leather jacket was draped over a wire-thin frame, sleeves rolled up at the cuffs. "Cup of coffee, any way you want to make it. You got a pencil I could borrow?" His voice had an almost melodic quality to it, carrying through the stiff morning silence like birdsong on the wind. His dark eyes - matching almost with his skin - twinkled at her, a lone light in the dulled diner.

Katherine nodded, slipping him the pencil she kept in her apron pocket before turning, grabbing a mug from the dish rack and the coffee pot from the rusted Bunn.

When she sat the mug down in front of him - the diner's mugs sculpted by Tony's once-brilliant hands - he was scribbling something on a napkin, holding it taught with one hand while scrawling with the other. He didn't seem to notice her. She sat down a handful of creamers. Still, he didn't look up, and the pencil kept on moving.

She cleared her throat. Still, nothing. He seemed to her a man in a dream, a man possessed. His hand kept moving, his eyes never leaving the napkin, his lips held slightly open as if in a prolonged sigh.

"Sir?" She asked, a bit louder, a gunshot in the still diner. He startled, so she startled, and almost dropped the pot of coffee.

He folded the napkin up as she poured him his coffee, slipping it into an inside pocket of his jacket.

"Sorry about that," the man said with a half-grin. "I uh, tend to get a bit too into the 'zone,' if you know what I mean."

Katherine breathed out a laugh. "What're you writing?"

The man smiled again, and this time there was nothing half about it. "Oh, the question that writers hate. If I could tell you, I would, ma'am. It was just words that the wind brought to me - and who am I to deny the wind?"

"Fair enough, stranger." She leaned on the counter, this time toward him. No one else was in the diner - and wouldn't be, not until Mr. Dunrow came in at eight o'clock on the dot, as he always did, for his cup of coffee (two creams, one sugar) and a double to-go order of eggs for him and Ms. Betty.

No, no one would be in for quite some time, and Katherine could use a story or two to keep her company - Lord knew that there were few enough of those to go around anymore in Billings.

"Where're you coming from anyway, stranger?" A look at his license plate would have given her more than a hint, but she didn't have to look there to know that he wasn't from anywhere near Billings. No one there - and Katherine knew just about everyone in the town - could afford a car like that.

The man took a sip of his coffee, both hands wrapped around the mug. "I was an editor for a small-time newspaper in Nowhere, Illinois. Live in a backwater town long enough and you start to feel like backwater yourself. Wasn't doing too good for me up here," here he tapped the side of his head with the pencil. "I was suffocating in that town - I mean, I couldn't even tell you the last time I had written something, created something that was just for myself. I couldn't breathe in that town, so one day I just started driving and driving, and..." He laughed a little, taking another sip of his coffee. "Well, I got to Chicago before I realized that I'd left my wallet at home."

Katherine laughed too. She liked this man - the Route drew in every sort of person from off the road, and he was better than most. He was a breath of fresh air into this musty town, and for the first time she realized that the murals still had that life to them, though the sun had long since risen out of the windows.

"So what's this town like?" He met her eyes, and she could see that the question wasn't one of nicety - it was genuine.

"Why, you thinkin' of moving here, stranger?"

He let out another one of those laughs, shrugging. "Like to keep my options open. Can't stay on the road forever."

What was Billings like? She'd lived there for every one of her twenty-four years - except for the summer stay in Wichita that had turned into a year-long venture with her cousins. She was born here. She'd died a half-death here when her momma had passed a few years back. She'd probably die again in a few more years, long after this stranger had passed along and long after all of the diner's regulars had passed into the same faded memory as the murals.

She'd had dreams once. Everyone in this town had had dreams once.

You didn't come to Billings to fulfill those dreams, not the American one and certainly not ones you kept tucked under your pillow and thought about when the summers were too hot to do just about anything and whispered under your breath when things went from bad to worse and your daddy came home drunk again and you wished that you could be somewhere where those dreams could be made real.

So what was Billings like? Katherine supposed she could tell him about Tony and his paintings - Tony, who'd once done murals on the sides of the General Motors plants until the economy tanked and that too had closed up, and who'd done face painting at the church fair every year until they couldn't afford to keep it up and no one in town had enough to help. Tony, who Katherine would probably find when the breakfast rush started, slumped and asleep on his office desk, one hand clutching a cigarette that had long since put itself out.

Instead she turned around - with the intention to wash more mugs but with no real want to - and simply said. "Not too different from the backwater you came from, I'll reckon."

The bell of the diner chimed, again and again. The day was starting out to be a busy one, and Katherine barely spoke again to the stranger, except for him asking her for a plate of eggs and if it would possibly be alright if he took up a booth near the back for the day, and her telling him that they'd be out in a jiff and a half, and that she had no control over his life, of course he could. This last part was said with a half smile that she couldn't remember slipping on to her face and that she didn't think came off until her shift was done.

The day was a busy one, but a good one. It would have been pointless to say that all the regulars came in, because the only people that came into Tony's *were* regulars. Mr. Dunrow was first, surprisingly with little Ms. Betty in tow. They ate their eggs in the diner that morning, which was a welcome surprise to Katherine. Then came Jim, the banker who lived up on East Street, and his boy. Rita and Jo, the friends from the nursing home, and Charlie, on his break from the machine shop, smelling as he always did - a mixture of sweat, cigarette smoke, and oil.

She didn't talk to the stranger, no, but that smile lingered on her face. *When was the last time I smiled like that?*

It wasn't that she was sad, per se, but it was almost like there had been no time or space for happiness. Few of her friends stayed in the area for college, and fewer still came back to visit. And after her momma died, Katherine had found it easier to focus on the diner and on taking care of her withering father than to think about any sort of frivolities that she couldn't afford, emotionally or monetarily. And at the end of the day, when she was mopping the kitchen, a thought came to her so suddenly that she stopped in the middle of a puddle, letting the mop drench her shoes in dirty soap.

The thought was this: Katherine hadn't painted since her momma had died. No, it was more than that - she hadn't thought about painting at all since her momma died, and (and this was the part that caused her to stop in her tracks) she hadn't given her forgetfulness a second thought since then. Not until now.

Tony nearly slipped as he walked into the kitchen, letting out a curse and muttering (if you could call his volume a mutter) about how absentminded she was, and if the old folks didn't love her so much she would have been fired long ago.

Katherine didn't hear him. She looked at him like a woman in a daze, leaning on the mop like it was a crutch. "Tony," she asked, her eyes fixed on his. "Do you remember those art lessons you used to give me when I was a kid?"

"Sure, why?" Those classes had been in this kitchen on Tuesday evenings on the stainless steel table she had just scrubbed, whenever her momma had been able to afford them and even when she hadn't. Katherine had never noticed how gray Tony's eyes were - like a blank sky just moments before dawn colored its heavenly slate.

She felt herself snap back to herself. "No reason. Was there something you needed back here?"

"Yeah," he said, coughing into a closed fist. That damn smoker's lung. "That kid from this morning was asking for you."

Katherine leaned the mop against one wall, wiping her hands on a towel as she went back out front. There he was, his leather jacket slung over his shoulder as he leaned over the counter, a mirror image of his figure that morning superimposed onto a background of dusk.

"What can I do for you now, stranger?"

He gestured to the plate and coffee cup he had brought to the counter. "Just cleaning up. Could I get a coffee for the road? I don't know how long I'm going to need to stay up."

A coffee at nine o'clock? Those Chicago types sure were something. "All I've got left is cold, but if you want it, it's yours."

"However you made it this morning was perfect," he said with that half-grin.

She handed him his cup and wished him safe travels. "I'll try my best," he replied in harmony with another half-grin. Did two half-grins make a whole one? Katherine thought so. "The tip's on the table." He turned toward the door, pausing only when his angles were framed by the doorway and backlit by the fluorescence of the diner. "Thanks for talking this morning. Don't get that too much along the road."

Katherine watched him walk out to his car, that beautiful Camaro, before she went to his table. A few crumpled fives were folded over themselves. There was something else folded in with them, she realized. A napkin, with something scrawled messily onto it.

It was the napkin from that morning, the one the stranger had been so enraptured with. It took her a moment to decipher the writing on it. It was verse, she realized.

Why didn't anyone tell me that rose petals were as
soft as velvet?
Or that a flock of finches is
called a charm?
What a life to live!
What a road to travel!

Katherine stood for a moment, the headlights of the Camaro casting a halo about her before the stranger turned out of the parking lot and back onto the road.

What a life to live, she thought to herself. "So why aren't I living it?" She asked out loud, to no one in particular - except maybe the murals.

"You say something?" Tony poked his head out from the kitchen.

Katherine turned quickly, shoving the napkin and the crumpled bills into her pocket. She hurriedly undid the lace of her apron, tossing it down onto the table.

"I've got to go, Tony. Now." Ignoring his sputterings that there was still work to do, and promising to be in early the next day, Katherine strode out into the warm night, got into her tan station wagon with a crack in the driver's side window, and drove home.

Her house was a lonely one, though it was surrounded on each side by rows of other houses. She knew she'd find her daddy passed out on the couch, she knew she'd find a stack of dishes collecting water in the sink - and she knew where she'd find her painting supplies.

She turned the doorknob to her mothers bedroom. She hadn't been in here since before her momma had been taken to the hospital. She couldn't have before, but tonight she could. And she did.

Dragging an easel and canvas into her own room and cracking her window so the fumes didn't get to her, she began. She wasn't paying attention to what she was painting, exactly, or how she was feeling. She wasn't paying any attention at all.

She simply created. *I couldn't even tell you the last time I had created something,* the stranger had said.

I couldn't remember the last time I felt alive, Katherine thought.

It wasn't until her daddy started crashing around downstairs and that perfect glow of morning shone through her window did she realize what she had made.

It was him - though she had painted him facing outward, she knew it was him. The stranger.

Facing the road, that sunrise that she craved bathing him in a halo of soft light. His pose suggested freedom, and Katherine felt more free than she had in a long time.

A part of her - the part that burned to create - had died with her momma. But another part - the part that weighed her dreams down with complacent lethargy - had died that morning, when that crimson Camaro had come roaring up the road.

In the place where the old Katherine had died, a new one was born. One who had dreams again - but more importantly, one who could see all the dreams that could be realized right here in Billings once the gray filter was removed and replaced with a vibrant dawn, full of color and light and life.

What a world she lived in! She could see that now.

What a road she could travel! She had already taken the first step.

About the Author

Zak Burns is a junior in high school from Farmington Hills, MI. He has been passionate about storytelling since a young age, when he realized that LEGO was the perfect vehicle to tell the stories he didn't quite yet know how to write. He plays the viola and the guitar, is an avid table-top gamer and is involved with his school's theater program. He enjoys reading fantasy books as well as every flavor of horror. He most likes to write about people and the stories they can tell.

Teen Readers' Choice Winner
Some Things That We Hide
Joyce Tchuente

Nineteen year old Julius had a reason. For all the hair that was piling on the corners of his bathroom wooden floors and porcelain countertops. Casualties of nervous fingers. This was how things had always been in his world: late night sessions of deep pondering matters of the foreseeable future accompanied by the routined plucking of hairs from his scalp. Silent battles fought in front of the mirror. But today felt different. Today he would make a dent in his world, even if it was by… looking normal.

He lifted the razor to his head, dragging it over the patchy surface on his head. If he didn't look in the mirror, he wouldn't have to see what he'd done. He had changed. And change was scary, sure, but going to his first day of work to showcase his usual self in fragments would've been worse.

Maybe taking a questionable alleyway hadn't been the most rational way to get to *24/7 Mart* at 7:30 am in the morning, but here he was. The brick walls he stood in between were packed with color. *Graffiti*. Its Rigid, bubbly, and curvy letters expressed themselves in ways and languages that Julius had once studied in high school. He paused, eyes tracing the sharp colors, lingering on a piece that stopped just short of a word – maybe forgotten, maybe unfinished. He pulled himself from the alley and toward the bright, buzzing sign of 24/7 Mart. To the right of the door, a small "open" sign hung, a quiet invitation. Julius had taken a second to brace himself for whatever waited inside. Stepping in, he was struck by the cool fluorescent light that panged his eyes and head. As he approached the front counter to ask where he should start, he spotted a kid– well not exactly a kid, but just young enough to be mistaken for one. The guy sat behind the front register, casually as ever, rotating side to side on a swivel chair.

"Uh, hi. I'm Julius Minda, Here for my first day as cashier?" He hadn't meant for it to come out as a question but he would be lying if he didn't admit that he was a little confused.

"Julius! Yes!" The young blonde perked up, slurring together the S's he had pronounced, "Mr. Bill told me-agh to be your guide today!" He walked to the back of the store before Julius had the chance to respond.

He returned with a navy blue vest, matching the one that he wore.

"H-here, wear this" he pointed to his name tag, "I'm Theo by the way. Y..you'll get one of these by tomorrow."

Julius had noticed Theo's stutter as he then slipped on the stiff blue vest. The vest was too big, making the shoulders droop awkwardly. He ran his fingers over the empty name tag spot. "Nice. Looks like I'm drowning in professionalism."

Theo grinned, catching the comment. "Don't worry. By tomorrow, you'll blend right in." He glanced down, "Well, uh, unless you wear socks like those every day." Julius felt his ears burn as he remembered his mismatched socks—one a bright green, and the other a striped black and white.

"Ah, yeah," Julius said, forcing a chuckle. "Fashion statement. I'm starting trends nobody asked for."

Theo spun in the chair once before hopping off. "Bold, I like it. Come on—I'll show you to the, uh, breakroom, then we'll go over the b-basics. Sounds good?" Julius nodded, trailing behind as Theo led the way to the back. He kept his head down, avoiding his reflection in the freezer doors they passed. The subtle outline of his freshly shaved head flashed in the corner of his eye, and he had to force his hand away from his scalp before he started tugging again.

In the breakroom, Theo plopped into a chair, immediately spinning again. "Okay, so rule number one: if someone tries to pay in all coins, prepare to hate your life. Rule number two—"

"Wait," Julius interrupted. "That's it? No 'don't steal, no 'be nice to customers'?"

Theo stopped spinning, an exaggerated look of seriousness on his face.

"Look, man. If you can survive coin customers, you can survive anything. L-life lessons right there."

That got a laugh out of Julius. Small, but real.

The register was older than Julius expected, with buttons that looked like they'd been smashed with generations of impatient fingers. Theo leaned against the counter, one hand still on the swivel chair he'd wheeled for himself.

"Okay so, disclaimer for the register: no sudden m-movements," Theo said, pressing a button carefully, "This thing has… trust issues."

Julius smirked as he went through the basics: scanning items, punching in prices, and making change. He felt himself relaxing a little. Theo was easy to talk to and maybe he wouldn't dread his time here as much. Julius even caught himself nodding along to Theo's rant about how people shouldn't bring expired coupons if they didn't want to be gently but surely judged.

A customer came by with a bag of chips and an energy drink, bringing Julius out of his thoughts. Theo motioned for him to take the lead.

"Go on," Theo said, tapping his shoulder. "Y-ou've got this."

Julius hesitated, his hands hovering awkwardly over the register. The customer, an older man with a baseball cap pulled low over his eyes, he looked impatient but said nothing.

"Uh…" Julius muttered, fumbling to scan the chips. The barcode wouldn't register. He could feel his fingers stumble.

"Here," Theo said calmly. He reached over and angled the chips slightly. "Sometimes the scanner's… picky. Try now."

The beep finally came, and Julius exhaled as he scanned the energy drink. "$4.52," he said, glancing up nervously. The man paid in cash, and Julius handed over the change effortlessly.

As the man walked away Theo commented, "Not so bad," he brushed off his vest, "And hey, bonus points for not letting the guy's vibe throw you off. I've seen him argue over pennies before."

Julius snickered, shaking his head. "I don't think I've ever concentrated so hard on a bag of chips."

"Eh, f-first shifts are like that," Theo said, "Soon, you'll be scanning stuff in your sleep," He scratched his chin, "And somehow I still wake up feeling underpaid."

Julius leaned against the counter, feeling a little lighter. "You're interesting."

"Takes one to know one, you know, m-mismatched socks" Theo shot back, spinning fast on his chair, "you're pretty interesting too."

Julius opened his mouth to respond but hesitated. He was about to deflect with a joke. But the lighthearted conversation just cooled him down, so he shrugged, a small smile tugging at his lips.

"Maybe," he said. "Guess I'm still figuring that out."

Theo stopped spinning, his expression relaxing. "Aren't we all?"

The store quieted as the afternoon stillness set in, leaving Julius and Theo with nothing but the hum of fluorescent lights and the occasional ding from the automatic doors. Theo leaned back in his chair, balancing on its leg.

"You're settling in," Theo said, his voice casual. "Not bad for a, uh, first day."

Julius shrugged, toying with the corner of his navy vest. "Yeah, I guess. No big disaster yet."

"Low bar, but it's still progress," Theo responded. He thought for a moment then added, "Y..you know, when my first day started, I thought I would get fired. Had this customer who didn't let me finish a s-sentence before they stormed off. Thought I was done for."

Julius looked at him, surprised. "Because of your stutter?"

Theo nodded, rocking on the chair gently. "Yeah. It's been like that my entire life. P-people think it's annoying or that I'm nervous, or even just dumb. Used to bother me a ton."

Julius stayed quiet, sensing that there was something more.

"But then I realized," Theo continued, "who cares? I s-still do what I love. I play basketball. I talk to people. I spin in, uh, chairs." He flashed a grin, but his tone softened. "It's just me, you know?"

Julius nodded slowly. He looked down at his hands, where his nails dug into his palms. "I guess… I have something like that too," he said, his voice quieter.

Theo tilted his head curiously. "I have this thing called trichotillomania," he said, wanting it to seem more like a conversation than a confession. "It's.. I pull my hair out. I don't even realize I'm doing it. It just sort of happens."

Theo's face didn't change. No judgement, no pity, just general interest. "That's why you shaved your head?"

"Yeah. I figured it'd help me stop, or at least hide it better. But it's not just the hair. It's everything that comes with it. The feeling of control. I don't want to seem broken."

Theo tapped his fingers on the edge of the counter, thinking. "You're not broken," he said simply. "You're just s-special. And it's not bad. It's just… special." Theo shrugged, " I mean, look at me. I trip over half my words, and I still talk too much. But it doesn't stop me from b-being me. And you? You're funny and sharp." He pointed at Julius clumsily, "You're more than just the stuff you think holds you back."

Julius felt a smile tug at his lips. "Thanks, Doc."

Theo grinned. "Anytime. That'll be $4.52, plus tax."

The two of them laughed and for the first time in what felt like forever, Julius didn't feel like he had to hide. And doors continued to ding for more customers, scanners kept failing, and change kept spilling but Julius finally felt that maybe, just maybe, things could get better.

About the Author

Joyce Tchuente is an artist, athlete and occasional writer who finds joy in bringing stories to life whenever inspiration strikes. A dedicated bookworm, she wrote this story to explore her passion for storytelling. When she's not writing or creating, Joyce enjoys gliding across the ice rink, traveling to new places and spending quality time with her family.

Teen Published Finalist

Passenger Planes and Burning Buildings
Kate Messina

September 2018

"September 11, 2001. The day that changed our world forever."

I pause, biting my lip as I study the date written on the whiteboard in neon orange marker. Behind me, twenty restless seventh-graders wait for me to continue my lecture, but when I open my mouth, the words don't come.

The images do.

Passenger planes.

Burning buildings.

Screaming citizens.

"The day...that changed our world forever," I repeat.

The day that changed...my world forever.

I turn to face the class, take a deep breath, and resume: "Seventeen years ago today, our nation experienced a tragedy not seen since the 1941 attack on Pearl Harbor."

I've barely finished when the girl in the front of the class, Sam Beck, pauses in her notetaking and raises her hand.

"Yes, Sam?"

"How old were you on September 11, 2001?" she wonders. The other kids groan, anticipating a new lecture tangent.

In my mind's eye, I see an innocent college freshman with a steady GPA and big dreams for her future. "I...I was eighteen."

"Did you see the attacks?"

I look down at my lecture notes, overtaken by the memories once more.

Clouds of dust.

Flashing emergency lights.

The wounded. The dying. The dead.

"I did."

Proceeding with my prepared lecture, I try to ignore Sam's assessing gaze, but it lingers on me until the bell finally rings and the seventh-graders stampede out of the classroom.

I sink into my chair and rub my temples. When I took this teaching position, I knew that at some point, I'd have to teach about this day. I knew it would be painful...but I hadn't expected it to hurt this badly.

Time heals, as they say. But it hasn't healed everything.

Someone shyly clears their throat. I glance up at Sam, who hovers by her desk.

"Can I help you, Sam?"

"I want to know more...about 9/11."

I can tell by the look on her face that she doesn't want the facts. She wants *my story.*

Reluctantly, I nod, and she drags her desk chair forward to sit opposite me. Once she's comfortable, I take a deep breath—and for the first time in forever, I tell my story.

The story of the day that not only changed the world...

...but that changed my life.

Seventeen years prior...

The ringing phone breaks the silence in my car. Jolting, I reach into the purse on my passenger seat and pull out my cell phone. *Mom.*

"Good morning, Chris," she says.

"Morning." I stop at a red light and wince as a taxi driver next to me lays on his horn, cussing out the semi-truck in front of him. A good New York City morning indeed.

"I need to ask you a favor," Mom pants. "Last night, I left my briefcase in your car after work...your dad drove me this morning, but we made it all the way to work before I remembered where I left it."

"Big meeting today?" The light turns green, and I inch forward in the bumper-to-bumper traffic.

"I'm giving four manuscripts to an editor for him to review. This could be my big break." Her tone brightens for a moment, but fades when she adds, "They're all in the briefcase, though. Any chance you can swing by before class?"

I check my watch. *8:30.* Class starts at 8:45, but I can risk missing one lecture to help Mom: after all, publishing her writing is a huge step for her. I'm just happy she can get back to doing what she loves after eighteen years of raising me.

"Where's your meeting?"

"The World Trade Center. I know it's out of your way..."

"No worries, Mom. On my way now."

"You're the best, Chris. I'll meet you outside the buildings."

"Happy to help. Love you."

"Love you."

After she hangs up, I squint at the nearest street signs: I'm about five minutes from college and roughly ten from the World Trade Center. I roll down my windows, letting in the crisp early-autumn breeze and the pungent aroma of car exhaust.

Ah, New York City. Vastly different from our hometown of San Diego, the Big Apple was a huge change for my family when my dad's job moved us here over the summer. However, we adjusted quickly and began to enjoy the city life; not to mention, we'd moved closer to my boyfriend of almost two years, Willem, who moved here last fall to start his paramedic degree at a local community college.

A text message buzzes against my thigh, as if on cue.

Hey, you! I'm off at 5 today—dinner and a movie?

I smile at Willem's cheery text and reply, Hey, you. It's a date. Being long-distance with Willem was tricky, but it made the move to the big city much sweeter.

I finally pull up to the Trade Center, and I peer up at the North and South Towers looming over the street and glinting in the sunlight. While I drive past, searching for a parking spot, I glimpse Mom, standing just outside the North Tower, looking professional in a blazer and flared pants. She looks poised, confident, ready for anything.

I've just located an area without a "no parking" sign when the roar of a jet engine scatters my thoughts, and a massive passenger plane streaks out of the heavens, colliding with the North Tower.

I slam the brake and jerk my car into park. Behind me, cars collide with crashes to rival the deafening explosion on the Tower. I gawk at the dense black smoke billowing from the side of the skyscraper. People scramble out of their vehicles and clog the road, running, screaming, standing, staring in utter shock. Debris rains down—chunks of glass and steel and stone—like a deadly, flaming hail.

All I can think about is the bold, brave woman waiting for me outside.

I want to get out of my car, I want to look for her, but I'm terrified, frozen in place be hind the steering wheel. This is just a nightmare. Any minute, I'll wake up.

My phone rings. I shake myself and answer it.

"Chris," Dad's tone is steady and urgent.

"Dad, did you see?" My voice rises in volume as I speak. "Dad, the Tower—Mom—the people—the plane—"

"Calm down," he commands. "Listen to me. Where are you?"

"Outside. Outside the building." I look up. Drifting smog blocks out the sun. *Where's Mom?*

"What building?"

"The—the North one."

"The Trade Center?"

I take a frantic breath, eyes scanning the base of the tower. People stream out of the dark cloud of smoke.

"Christina. Talk to me."

"Mom needed her briefcase." I border on hysteria. "What do I do? What—"

"Get out of there."

Sirens announce the arrival of first responders: policemen, firefighters, EMS workers.

"You need to leave, Chris. Go home and stay inside."

"Dad, I can't." I watch as paramedics and firefighters rush toward the flaming building.

All I can think is, *Find my mom. Save my mom. Please.*

More bodies fill the streets. More chaos ensues.

"You need to."

"I can't," I repeat. Pressed in by the heavy traffic, I'm backed against the curb with cars in front of and behind me. "I'm fenced in."

Silence. Then a deep, heavy sigh. "Just stay where you are, and don't leave the car. I'm almost there."

Without another word, he hangs up.

And once more, I'm alone. Afraid. Desperate.

Time drags. 9:00 comes and goes, and I can't stop thinking of Mom and her big dreams and her big meeting. *Where is she?* At 9:03, another ominous roar echoes among the buildings—a second plane swerves from the sky and crashes into the South Tower.

I scream. I scream because I can't control the situation, I scream because they still haven't found my mom, I scream because of the implications of this second impact.

It's no longer an accident.

This was *planned.*

I'm still frozen in fear when movement on the sidewalk catches my eye.

I turn just as my passenger door swings open and my dad climbs in.

"Chris," he attempts, before I burst into tears. I find myself wrapped in his fierce embrace. I think of days long since past where one hug from Dad could make the world seem right again. Except this time, the world doesn't seem right again.

"Dad, Mom was right there. She was outside, waiting for me..." I trail off, holding back another wave of tears. By the emotions tearing across Dad's face, I know he's coming to the same conclusion as me. He closes his eyes for the briefest of moments—then he just gets out of the car, and I follow.

It's worse out here, with frightened people everywhere. The movement around me is dizzying. Tension hangs heavy in the air as people bustle around and emergency forces dart in and out of the buildings. I want to join them, to search the wreckage for a familiar face, but Dad's firm hand on my shoulder holds me back.

There are so many bodies. Wounded. Mutilated. Dead. I shut my eyes to block out the terrible sights.

Please, Mom. You can't go. You're not allowed to go.

Dad squeezes my shoulder, and I look up. He nods in the direction of the nearest ambulance, and I follow his gaze hopefully. My heart sinks. It's not Mom.

But...it's him.

Covered in soot, his paramedic uniform torn and scorched, he carries a limp woman to the back of an ambulance, watching wearily as other paramedics sweep her away for better care. Then, he looks up.

Our eyes meet.

I don't even remember running. But I'm pushing past the bystanders and squeezing between crumpled cars until I stumble into his arms. He's shaking, covered in dust, but here. Warm and alive and *here.*

"Willem."

"Chris." His heartbeat pounds against my cheek. He buries his face in my hair.

Here, in Willem's firm and comforting hold, my tears finally spill over.

"Willem, my mom—" I gasp into his shirt. "She was standing—and then—oh, what happened?"

"I don't know." He pulls away and studies the smoking towers. "This isn't a mistake, Chris. Somebody did this."

"But who?"

"I don't know." His voice shakes, and now I see the anguish in his eyes. He wants to help. He wants to save every life. But at this moment, he knows he can't. I can't imagine how that must feel.

A foreboding rumble suddenly quakes the street. People scream and point up at the South Tower. Willem follows their gestures, and his mouth falls open.

"Run." He suddenly grabs my hand and pulls me along as he weaves between the cars, away from the buildings. "Chris, run."

I can barely move, let alone run. A vast cloud of black dust and debris surrounds the South Tower as it seems to be...*shrinking.*

No. Not shrinking. *Collapsing.*

I bump into the side of a car. "Willem—"

"Come on!" We're swept along by the crowd pushing through the jumble of automobiles and debris. I search for my dad in the mob, but I can't see a thing past the panicked masses. Behind us, the debris cloud grows, swallowing entire skyscrapers, moving faster than the citizens can, enveloping firefighters, paramedics, businessmen, moms and dads and little kids.

"Here!" Willem yanks open the rear door of a nearby sedan and drags me into the backseat, slamming the door behind us. Almost instantly, the blizzard of grime and wreckage sweeps over the vehicle, turning the windows tan. Wind whistles past as Willem and I sit, gasping for air. I can't see a thing outside, but I can picture the scene of suffering. A lump rises in my throat, but I just whimper. Willem wordlessly wraps me in his arms and holds me while the cloud moves past outside.

"My mom, Will," I whisper. "My dad..."

"I know," he replies, leaning his forehead on my shoulder.

Sudden static makes us both jump. We stare at the walkie-talkie clipped to Willem's belt as a deep, husky voice crackles through the device.

"Davies, you there?"

Willem's hands shake as he raises the apparatus to his mouth.

"I'm here."

"We need your help by the towers. Lots of trapped people."

"On my way." And just like that, Willem's about to open the door.

"Wait! Wait, Will." I grab his arm, and he turns to look at me, frowning. "Please, don't go. Don't leave me."

"I'll let them know where you are. Someone will find you, okay?"

"Who? When? Don't leave, please." I'm sobbing again, holding to him for dear life because if he leaves, I fear I'll lose him, too.

"I have to help." He leans in and kisses me. It feels bittersweet, like... like goodbye.

Tears shine in his eyes when he pulls away.

"I love you."

"I love you, too." My voice is scarcely a whisper. He cuts off the end with another quick kiss, then he pushes out into the street.

A swirl of dust remains where he used to be.

I curl up on the backseat and cry. I cry for Mom. I cry for Dad. I cry for Willem. I cry for the terrified strangers on the streets. I cry until I can't cry anymore, and then I fall asleep.

"Ma'am. Ma'am, are you alright?"

Groggily, I lift my head from the cold leather seat, struggling to get my bearings.

A man waits for me with the car door open. It's dark outside. What time is it?

Everything comes back at once.

Mom.

Dad.

Willem.

I burst into tears again, and next I know, the man carries me through the unrecognizable streets of New York City, still shrouded in a heavy veil of dust and smoke.

Where the Twin Towers used to be, only rubble remains. Firemen and paramedics pick through the mess, dragging injured survivors out left and right.

Paramedics. *Willem.*

"My boyfriend," I say as the man sets me on the back of an ambulance. "Willem Davies. He...he came back here..."

The man exchanges a look with one of his coworkers. My heart skips a beat.

"No. No, no, no."

"Ma'am, you need to stay calm," he attempts.

I can't stay calm. "Where are my parents—Lydia and David Lewis? Please, I need to find them."

More movement. More voices. I hear Willem's name—these men and women knew him. They worked with him. They loved him. I repeat my questions, but they just wrap me in blankets and pat my shoulder consolingly.

As they bustle around me, I quiet, and I watch while they bring in new patients and softly discuss more losses.

I'm not the only one who's lost everything today.

"Chris." Dad is here. I climb out of the ambulance and wobble into his open arms. Distantly, I hear him talking to the paramedics, but I only catch bits and pieces.

"Still finding bodies...confirmed loss...Lydia...deceased."

"Dad..." I peer up at him, but he's shaking his head, confirming my worst fears.

No more dreams of published books and big breaks.

No more lives saved and dinner dates arranged.

I check my watch. Past the broken screen, I read 5:01 p.m.

We should have been eating dinner now, laughing over a New York style pizza or slurping ramen noodles.

The tears return when Dad thanks the paramedics and starts to lead me away. "No! Please, please, there has to be something we can do!" I plead with the paramedics. They watch me with a strange mixture of regret and empathy. "Please," I attempt, my voice breaking. "I want them back. I *need* them back. You don't understand..."

Tears shine on Dad's cheeks, too, as he gently pulls me away from the calamity. I want to shriek and fight and run back into the mess to prove the paramedics wrong...but deep down, I know they're right.

"It'll be okay, Chris," Dad says as he leads me away.

The growing ache in my chest reminds me that everything is not, in fact, okay. Everything's changing.

And nothing—nothing at all—will ever be the same again.

Present Day

I take a shuddering breath and lean back in my desk chair, crossing my arms. In the background, the bell rings, signaling the end of the school day.

Sam gasps, tears leaking from under her glasses. I hand her a tissue.

"So, Willem? And...and your mom?"

I nod slowly. She sobs into her tissue.

"Aw, Sam," I murmur.

"I can't imagine," she whispers. "H-how did you keep going?"

I frown. I don't know how I made it through the sleepless nights, the nightmares, the funerals. I don't know how I endured the barrage of memories that leapt out from every photo frame. I don't know how I survived the pain of calling down the hall for Mom before remembering she wasn't there or checking for good morning texts that would never come.

I think the only reason I survived...was for them. Because of them, their memories, their legacies. The love they left behind spurred me on to where I am today.

The smile I offer Sam is sad, yet grateful.

"I kept going because I knew they would want me to."

They would have wanted me to be strong. So, for them, I was strong.

Sam smiles back, and I know she understands.

"Thank you, Ms. Lewis," she says, standing to collect her things. "For telling me."

"No, Sam," I reply. "Thank you. For listening."

As she pads out of the classroom, I glimpse the photos in the frame next to my pencil holder—photos I haven't stopped to look at in far too long.

The paramedic with the cocky grin.

The laughing, innocent girl at his side.

The parents, beaming, without a care in the world.

The perfect life I knew before one day changed my world forever.

About the Author

Kate Messina is a high school senior who has always loved writing. Through random bursts of inspiration—often drawn from music, games played with her younger sisters and even other books—she crafts her concepts whenever she gets the chance . . . if her Pinterest boards and Spotify playlists don't distract her first. When not writing (or avoiding writing), she can normally be caught singing, drawing, reading, scrapbooking, composing music and spending time with the family and friends who never cease to inspire her characters' adventures.

Teen Published Finalist

Music
Natalie Koepke

"Go out into the woods and listen. Listen to the leaves rustling... the birds chirping... the stream flowing... There is music in everything, if only you listen." That was what my Grandfather had told me since the first day he had balanced me on his knee. That was what he had told me as I toddled across the leaf-strewn earth on little baby legs, as I learned to climb the old pine tree, as I ran across the dewy grass to pick wildflowers. "Remember, Autumn - there is music in everything." That was also the last thing he said to me, and it was the last music I ever heard. I was seven years old.

Two sisters and one brother came after me. One sister forgot the music, and the others were too young to remember it. So they grew up and built their own lives around their own personalities. Laura went to dances and hung out with friends, while Kyle worked alone in the workshop. Charlotte, the most athletic of us, ran track, played basketball, and did gymnastics competitively. I had nothing. My life had been built around music, and without it, nothing interested me. I envied my siblings for their blissful lives without the music I so missed. After all, it is easier to live without knowing what you're missing than to spend forever looking for what was lost, and never finding it.

I tried learning piano, and worked hard at it for nearly five years, until I was playing Chopin and Bach and Mozart with relative ease. But it was never real music, not in the sense that I remembered. When my teacher told Mama, "Autumn plays the notes, but her music has no life," I decided it was time to quit. Mama said I just needed practice, but that wasn't the problem. Music doesn't happen just because you play the right notes - it has to come from inside.

So it was that two weeks into November, during my fourteenth year, I was out of options. "Are you going to the Fall Dance with Laura and her friends?" Mama asked as she came into the room.

I looked up from my book. "I'm no good at dancing. And I don't fit in with Laura and her friends. It's not any fun."

"Autumn, sweetheart..." Mama sat down beside me and ran a hand through my auburn hair. "You don't need to fit in. You're special just the way you are. Don't worry about being like Laura - be like Autumn."

"Who is Autumn?" I asked. "Laura is the social one, Kyle is the artistic one, Charlotte is the athletic one... I was the musical one. I had music once, and now I don't have anything."

"You're also the intelligent one, and the thoughtful one, and the kind one," Mama said.

"I don't care," I whispered. "I want my music back."

"Do you want to try piano lessons again?"

I shook my head. "That's not what I meant. I can listen to music, or play music, but it's not the same. There's no music inside me. When Grandfather died, the music died with him."

"Oh Autumn..." Mama seemed at a loss for words. Finally she said, "Your grandfather - my papa - was a very special man. And when I think of him, I feel music. The music didn't die with him - it lives on in me. And in you."

"No," I said, closing my book. "Maybe there's music in you. But I have no music." Then I stood and left the room.

That was Friday afternoon, November 15th. A few hours later, we saw headlights coming toward the house, and three figures stepped out of their trucks, rifles in hand. They came inside a few minutes later, laughing and smiling, their coats stiff with cold. "Any luck?" Kyle asked as we all gathered at the table for dinner.

"I saw a few does, but no bucks," Uncle Mike replied. Does were fair game for most hunters, but my family never shot them. Still, I loved hearing stories of times when does had walked right up to the hunters without realizing they were there.

"I might have seen one, but I couldn't get my gun up in time," Daddy added.

My cousin Luken smiled, taking off his thick gloves and hugging my mother. "I didn't see anything, but I could smell Aunt Mary's cooking. God bless the cook!"

Opening day was practically a holiday at our house. Every year on November 14th, Mama cooked the last of the venison steaks, and we prayed for good hunting. For the next week, supper would be a festive event, with lively stories and a large dose of laughter. After we ate, Aunt Eliza and Mama would wash dishes while Laura and I cleaned the countertops and the table. Charlotte and Kyle would get out the chessboard, and Luken would cheer them on. Then Daddy would get out his guitar or put on a CD. Tonight,

Daddy, Uncle Mike, and Luken would sit up late playing cards around the table, and be gone before I woke up Saturday morning. That week the house would already be overflowing with the life most people don't get until Thanksgiving. Hunting season was one of my favorite times of the whole year.

After we said grace, Daddy looked in my direction. "Autumn? Would you like to come sit with me tomorrow?"

"In the woods?"

"Yes. Would you like to come hunting?"

"I... I guess I could." It wasn't like I had any other plans, and I did love spending time with my father. "Sure. I'll come."

"Autumn, time to wake up." I blinked, confused. Then my eyes focused, and I saw Daddy standing over me. "Breakfast's ready," he whispered. "Meet us at the table."

I put on some warm clothes and tiptoed down the hall into the bright, cheerful kitchen. Mama and Aunt Eliza had gotten up early. Sausage was sizzling on the stove, and the room smelled of hot coffee and syrup. It seemed just like any other day, except that the sky was still dark, and there was a certain sense of solemnity mingled with the lively atmosphere.

Luken looked up from his plate of pancakes and grinned as I sat down. "Morning, sleepyhead. Eat up, it's nearly five!"

As we ate, Daddy and Uncle Mike told me what to expect, reminding me that you didn't always see a deer, and even if you did, you might not get a shot. "No matter how many layers of socks you put on, your feet will get cold," Luken added when they were finished.

When we finished, Daddy helped me into layer after layer of clothing until I felt like a giant marshmallow. Finally he slid a bright orange hat snugly over my ears. "Ready?" he asked.

"Ready."

The moon was still shining brightly as we walked out to the truck and drove into the woods behind our house - the woods where I had once heard music. I was suddenly worried. What if Daddy got his deer today, while I was watching? Would I ever be able to go back into the woods, having witnessed death within their boundaries?

While I worried, Daddy parked the truck on one of our small trails. "We'll walk from here," he whispered, leading me confidently into the woods. The blind was nearly invisible, built of dead tree branches and set at the foot of a huge maple. Daddy brushed a fresh coating of snow off the little bench, and we sat down.

"Now what?" I asked.

Daddy smiled. "Now, we wait."

So we waited. And waited. My hands and feet grew numb with cold, as Luken had predicted, and I looked around, trying to find something to take my mind off the nipping frost. Everything was still, except for snow spiraling down to the ground in a silent ballet, and a single woodpecker tapping out its rhythmic song on the side of a bare birch. One last leaf fluttered on a nearby oak, and the stars began to fade as the sun peeked over the horizon.

Then Daddy touched my arm and pointed. A lone doe was crossing the ridge across from us. She stopped and looked, and we sat there, as still as statues and as silent as the falling snow. She watched us, and time seemed to pause as her large brown eyes met mine. Finally, deciding we weren't a threat, the doe continued on. When she was gone, Daddy passed me a lemon drop. He returned to watching the treeline, and I returned to watching the world.

I saw a pair of squirrels chase each other up and down a tree. I noticed the deep green of the evergreens, and the watercolor palette of the brightening sky. I saw the bare limbs of countless trees framed against the pinks and blues of the dawn. I watched the snow, moving, always moving, as it danced with the little zephyrs of wind, up and down and all over the hill. And then the sun came up in all its glorious beauty, casting its dazzling rays across the barren hills and flooding the world with light... flooding it with music.

As I looked, as I listened, the music soaked into my body. It was everywhere. I could feel it in the playful antics of the squirrels, in the brilliant blue sky, and even in the cold fingers of Jack Frost, tugging at my fingers and toes. I wanted to shout for joy, to dance and to sing. After seven years, I had finally found the music!

That's when my gaze fell upon the ridge, and I saw the buck. Unlike the stories I had heard of previous hunts, this buck wasn't running. He wasn't chasing a doe, moving so quickly the hunter only got one shot. This buck came over the rise and stopped, just inside the trees. He was testing the air, waiting to see if it was safe to come out. He held his antlers proudly aloft, and stood there in majesty. There wasn't music in the buck... he was music.

Then the shot rang out. My hands flew to my ears, and the buck bolted. For a moment, I thought he had gotten away as he darted through the woods. But then I saw him stumble and fall, and I knew he wouldn't get up again.

Daddy stood up, and I followed suit, numb all over. Just a few minutes ago, that magnificent creature had been made of music, and now we had killed it. As we drew nearer, I saw him lying motionless, blood staining the snow. The music was gone. All the music was gone. No longer could I feel it in the playful zephyrs, or in the bare trees, or in the lone woodpecker. No longer could I feel the music that had so recently filled my heart, and I was not sure I would ever feel it again.

Then Daddy knelt by the deer, folded his hands, and began to pray. "I thank you, my Heavenly Father, Maker and Creator of all things, for guiding my hands and allowing me to take the life of this deer. I thank you for the nourishment it will provide to the family you have blessed me with. I thank you for giving me the patience to wait, and the silence of the forest to reflect. Lastly, I thank you for my daughter Autumn, who was able to come with me this morning. I pray that this gift you have given us may sustain us throughout the year. In Jesus's name I pray. Amen."

As I looked at the deer, at my father kneeling beside the deer, I heard the music again. And I realized that there was music in death as well as in life. Just as there was music in the song of a bird, there was music in the inanimate clefts of granite. Just as there was music in the deer as he stood on the ridge, there was music in the gift of meat God had given us. And, as I thought about it, just as there was music in the first cry of a newborn baby, there was music when my grandfather left the sorrows and cares of this world behind him. There was music in everything.

When we got home, I went over to the piano that had for too long served more as an ornament than a source of music. I ran my hands over the keys, and picked out the tune to Minuet in G Major, a simple piece by Bach which I had known for years. This time, as my fingers danced across the keys, the music came out with expression, with life. I filled my music with the music of the woods, with a song of life, and of death... a song of hope and new life.

Eight years later, I held my first child in my arms. Rosemary smiled as I held her up to the window, where the sky was once again painted in watercolor hues, and the grass sparkled with fading wisps of frost. As a blue jay alighted on the scarlet maple, I looked at my little daughter. She was too young to know what she was looking at, but she drank it all in with bright eyes. Too young to understand, perhaps, but not too young to love what she saw.

So I passed the words Grandfather had told me from the cradle on to his great granddaughter. "Go out into the woods and listen," I whispered. "Listen to the leaves rustling, the birds chirping, the stream flowing. There is music in everything... if only you listen."

About the Author

Natalie Koepke is fifteen years old and has been writing stories for as long as she can remember. When she's not working on her trilogy, she enjoys reading, exploring the Great Lakes State or making music with family and friends. She loves being homeschooled by her mother and is blessed to share the classroom with five younger siblings. Her dream is to become a published novelist and move to the Upper Peninsula. Soli Deo Gloria!

Teen Published Finalist

The Cow That Jumped Over the Moon
Lorna Garlets

The barred cell-door slammed behind the cow like a tocsin of doom. "And stay there!" a butterknife ordered before he left the dungeons, sliding on the end of his handle with uncanny stability. Alice jumped, as usual. She still wasn't used to talking cutlery.

A line of forks stood against the wall.

"You think you're so smart," Alice said, by way of addressing the silverware. Her only response was a series of loud snores. The forks were all asleep.

"Not that that helps me any." Alice's attempt to break through the last cell-door had nearly knocked her unconscious and had resulted in a large bruise.

An explosion of deafening barks erupted from the dark depths of her roomy new cell. Alice mooed in terror and crowded against the door. Finally, she glanced back warily and yelled, "Hey! You're not scaring anyone! What are you doing in my cell? Come out of there!"

A small dog with curly brown fur leapt into the light. Alice nearly jumped out of her skin. "What is wrong with you!?" she demanded.

"I'm sorry," said the dog. "Who are you? Why are you here?"

"Well..." Alice's voice was sarcastic. "I don't see why you have a right to know, but I got kidnapped by the inhabitants of Cutlery Castle..." She indicated the forks. "Because I trespassed three feet onto their land."

"Why in the name of Cowland would you do that?" the dog asked. "Nobody trespasses on the land of Cutlery Castle."

"No Cowlander knows anything about the Forest of Myths, much less its silly capital!" Alice snapped. "I was looking for the *Alath Qar dust.*"

"Why?"

Alice scowled. "Must you know everything? How about telling me your name."

"Petrova. Yours?"

"Alice. Now, do you know where the *Alath Qar* dust is, or not?"

Petrova snorted. "It's here, of course. In Cutlery Castle."

"Where?" Alice cried eagerly.

"Do you expect me to know? I still can't see why you want it."

Alice rolled her eyes. "Bethany Herdwin! Haven't you heard of her? She's the most famous cow ever! She lived here in the Forest of Myths, but then she discovered the *Alath Qar* dust of the Flying-Horses and used it to jump over the Moon! She landed in Cowland, and she's our nation's founder! Every year the cows have a festival for her."

"Huh," said Petrova. "She jumped over the Moon? Sounds like a myth to me."

"It's not! You said yourself that the dust exists. I will find it and jump over the Moon."

Petrova looked at her thoughtfully. "I had a plan to escape, but I couldn't do it alone. If you want the dust, I'll get us out of here, and I'll help you find it."

Alice considered a moment.

Nobody believed me when I said I would jump over the Moon, she thought, but I WILL prove them wrong!

"Consider it done," she said.

The cell door swung open.

"In the name of Fá Prongs, Queen of Cutlery, I bring a proclamation," announced a long and sharp bread knife.

A spoon recited, "As captives of the cutlery you will serve us as slaves."

The fork spoke again. "You will polish us, clean our castle, and obey our orders."

"You will—"

Petrova gave a loud snore.

"Show some respect!" screamed the spoon, jumping up and down in fury.

Alice snapped, "Your talk is boring. Free us."

"No!" the spoon countered.

Petrova growled.

While the cutlery was distracted, Alice acted. She charged forward. Instantly, dozens of the spoons and forks screamed and ran, or rather slid, away (being much too small to fight) while the knives advanced to attack.

Alice dodged but felt several painful pricks where the knives cut her legs. Petrova, meanwhile, snatched a struggling spoon in her mouth and followed in the path which Alice cleared.

Within moments they arrived at the dungeon door. Alice watched as Petrova proceeded to pick the lock with the spoon.

"Hurry!" she yelled.

"Luckily," said the dog through clenched teeth, "I am an expert at picking locks."

Unfortunately the knives were organizing themselves and Alice knew they might attack any moment. They charged. "Look out!" cried Alice.

"Keep them off a moment, will you?" Petrova said.

"I can't!"

Petrova ignored her.

Gathering her wits about her, Alice faced the cutlery. She tried to think of comforting things: home, and Mother, and the love she had once had. Until Mother had laughed at her. She had said Alice could never jump over the Moon. Alice naturally had become angry. No encouragement or kindness from her own Mother.

But once Mother had loved her. Perhaps she still did. Perhaps even now Mother was sorry for making fun of her.

But I will never, ever forgive her.

Alice was growing angrier and angrier. The loud clattering of an advancing army of spoons, forks, and knives brought Alice back to reality.

She boiled over. "Move it!" she shouted. Tears welled up in her eyes, though she didn't understand why. "Keep away! Back off!"

They were daunted a moment, but at a command from their leader, they approached again. As they marched, they began to chant.

"Knives-forks-spoons, knives-forks-spoons!" Faster and faster, like the rumble of thunder in the distance, drawing nearer and nearer. Soon they were upon her, slashing and prodding and chanting their song, over and over and over.

Alice did her best to fight back, kicking and stamping and fighting them away from Petrova as much as she could, but her legs were criss-crossed with cuts and she was beginning to fear that the fight was already lost when she suddenly heard the longed-for click behind her.

"I've got it open!" Petrova dropped the spoon and shot through.

Alice leapt around and sped away at Petrova's heels. They ran down the corridor. Scraping and rattling behind them proved that the army of cutlery was making chase.

"Where are we going?" Alice gasped.

"I don't know."

Up ramps, down passages they ran. They dodged past ancient statues and fearsome figures of horses. The utensils, however, were terribly fast. They were never far behind.

All of a sudden, the runaways dashed through a door and found themselves in a huge hall.

They sprang back to block the entrance of the hall. Massive though they were, the doors took only moments to shove securely into place.

"We're safe," Alice panted.

"Maybe," said Petrova. "I just hope there's not another way for *them* to enter."

However, it was likely that they were secure for the time being. The gloomy, empty hall was simply enormous; as far as the eye could see, there was no other entrance; nothing but crumbling white pillars and a smooth floor made of marble.

Except for one thing. In the midst of the pillars, a good distance away, a moonbeam shone through a gap in the vaulted ceiling, illuminating a huge table. Upon the table stood a silver bowl with a silver lid. Long chains, attached to the marble floor, held him captive in the darkness of night. Nearby stood a silver cat, with a fiddle upon his shoulder, playing a soft lullaby.

The two hurried down to the table.

The bowl said, "What are you doing here?"

Alice started. So bowls could also talk in this strange land. The cat smiled, and switched to a lively country dance.

"Are you the guardians of the *Alath Qar*?" Petrova inquired at once.

The bowl slammed his lid on tight. He scowled. "How did you know?"

"Oh, I just guessed. Mind if we borrow some?"

Alice looked at him pleadingly. "I need it! I must jump over the Moon. I will die if I don't!"

"No!" the bowl snapped. "Nobody may take *Alath Qar* dust unless they free me. The Flying-Horses locked me up. If you want to fly, I must be released first!"

"You see," the cat explained, "it was the dust which enabled Flying-Horses to fly, and they captured the bowl to hold it. Then they disappeared, taking the key with them. You shall have all the dust you like...if you free him."

Alice couldn't speak, couldn't think. She sank to the floor in dismay. Even Petrova was at a loss for words.

The bowl looked uncomfortable. "I mean, I'm sorry you can't jump over the Moon," he ventured.

"That's not the only reason!" Petrova growled. "We need that dust to escape!"

Alice heard none of it. Images were racing through her mind. First, of her family and friends scoffing her. Her journey through the forest rushed by, and her meeting with Petrova. Spoons, forks, and knives marched past.

One spoon in particular stood out. Why?

Now she saw herself charging the cutlery to escape the cell. All at once, everything slowed down. In slow motion Petrova ran forward, snatched a spoon, and dashed for the lock of the dungeon door.

At that moment, Alice jumped to her feet. Then she wheeled around, and galloped toward the hall door.

Petrova barked, "Alice! What are you *doing??*"

Alice was pulling open the doors. Voices echoed in the corridor. "Knives-forks-spoons, knives-forks-spoons!"

"Alice, STOP!" Petrova screamed, but the doors slammed and Alice was gone.

Alice's hooves beat on the hall floor. She was a soldier, going to battle, not knowing if she was going to come out alive.

She turned the corner.

Hundreds of forks, spoons, and knives confronted her. But that was not all. At their head loomed a terrifying sight. Alice yelped with horror.

A gigantic fork hulked over the army, a cruel expression creasing her silver face.

It was Fá Prongs, Queen of Cutlery.

"Ha, so here's the little escaper," boomed the ruler.

Alice's only reply was a squeak.

"Darling," she continued, "We ought to be friends. Come now, I have you cowed." She laughed patronizingly. "If you agree to join me...you know, wait on me, that sort of thing...I'll forgive you."

Forgiveness. The word brought a pang to Alice's heart.

"I've done nothing to you that calls for forgiveness!" Alice yelled.

"Is that so?" Fá Prongs inquired.

"I pity you!" Alice said. She paused, and prepared for what she was about to say. "You wouldn't ever forgive me. Not really. But here and now," she cried, "*I forgive you*, for everything you've done. I may never escape from here, but I will not die in hatred!" All her misery was bubbling out in a stream of words. "You've treated me terribly. But that does not justify resentment! Bitterness! Those will eat me away from the inside, destroying instead of healing. You will murder me, but forgiveness will never be forgotten!"

Fá Prongs' face twisted in rage. "Kill her!" she shrieked.

The army charged. Alice braced herself. Then, she shot forward.

"What are you doing?" Fá Prongs yelped in surprise.

Alice dashed into the midst of the cutlery and caught a spoon in her mouth. Then she ran back through the crowd. Knives leapt at her, but a pulsing feeling of wonder carried her on. Forgiveness! She easily outpaced the cutlery, and flew like a shooting star around the corner. To her surprise the hall doors were wide open. She slid to a stop just inside the doors.

"Alice!" Petrova panted. Alice saw that her friend had just finished propping open the doors. "I was just coming after you," Petrova added. "What were you doing?" She glanced fearfully down the hall.

Alice shoved the doors shut and let the spoon clatter to the floor. She stepped on it before it scurried away. "You did say you were an expert at picking locks, didn't you, Petrova?"

"Calm down!" Petrova was exasperated.

The spoon absolutely refused to hold still.

The cat stopped playing the fiddle and looked down at the spoon. "Spoon," he asked, "Would you like to be free?"

The spoon stopped struggling and looked up at the cat. "Free? From the Queen? Queen Fá Prongs?"

Alice glanced at the cat. "Yes," she said.

"Very much indeed!" The spoon no longer looked fierce, but dreamy, as if she was thinking of something she wanted very much but had no hope of winning. "How?"

"It's hard to explain," Alice said. "But if you hold still and let Petrova use you to pick the lock, I promise that you'll be free by this evening."

The spoon looked at her critically. "Cows never break promises," the spoon said. "I'll do it."

"Careful," Alice said as Petrova raised the spoon onto a level with the chain's large lock.

"Mm-hm," Petrova said. She stepped forward and fitted the spoon's handle into the lock. The bowl watched in anticipation. Slowly, Petrova turned the spoon. There was a quiet click, and the lock was open. Petrova set the spoon on the floor.

"Huh," the dog said. "I didn't think it would open that quickly. I guess it's just because it's so old."

The bowl, meanwhile, was doing a jig on the table. "I'm free-ee, I'm free-ee, I'm free-ee," he sang delightedly. Finally, however, he sobered. Addressing Alice, he said, "Dear heroine of mine, what is your plan? I will do whatever is your majesty's bidding."

Alice rolled her eyes. "Here's my idea. If you use some of your dust to carry me over the Moon, there will still be some left, right?"

"Indeed, my heroine, my paragon, my benefactor."

Alice doubted that some of these words were in the right context, but went on with her thought. "I propose that you use the rest of the dust for Petrova, the spoon, and yourself, to convey you to somewhere safe. Cat, I suppose you want to come as well?" The cat laughed. "I don't and I won't. The castle is home and I'm perfectly happy here. The cutlery doesn't bother me. Ha! I bother them."

"If you say so...Bowl, is there enough for the four of us?"

"Yes, certainly, my her—"

"Excellent. We'll leave now."

The cat played a haunting melody as the spoon dipped herself into the glimmering dust which the bowl revealed.

Petrova took the spoon in her mouth and from the height of the table sprinkled the dust all over Alice's coat.

Instantly Alice felt different. She felt like a balloon, or a cloud, airy and weightless.

She could tell that with the slightest bounce she could fly up to the Moon. Even without a bounce, if she tried. *I'm not sure I like this*, she thought.

She inched over to the bowl and picked up the spoon as gently as she could. She moved over to Petrova, who was waiting patiently on the floor, and dumped the dust onto her.

"Oh!" said Petrova. The dog hopped on her paws and flew ten feet. "Yikes," Petrova said as she floated back to the ground. Alice shivered.

Meanwhile, the bowl and the spoon had been dusted, and they too were ready to leave.

"You go first," said the spoon to Alice, pointing to the opening in the ceiling. Alice shook her head, giving a quavery smile. "No, I want you and the bowl to go first," she said. "You've done so much for us."

"Oh, thanks!" The spoon leapt rapturously into the air. "Come on!" she said to the bowl.

The bowl gave an indulgent smile. "Oh, happy to," he said. He was hopping from side to side in anticipation.

"Thank you for setting us free!" the bowl and the spoon exclaimed.

"Thank you!" the dog and the cow replied.

So the bowl and the spoon recited the final farewells and glided upward, up through the opening in the ceiling, until they vanished among the stars.

"Are you ready?" Petrova asked.

Alice gave no answer. When Petrova looked, she saw that Alice was staring at the sky in fear. "I can't," she said.

Petrova was astonished. "But this is what you've been waiting for, working for! Are you going to stop now?"

Alice glanced at her, then back at the distant full Moon. She was trembling. "We can find another way."

"No! There is no other way!"

The darkness was closing in. In the distance, hidden in the pillared hall, voices could be heard. What were they saying?

"Knives-forks-spoons! Knives-forks-spoons!"

Petrova looked into the black depths and saw torches, distant but growing brighter. The cutlery had found a way into the hall!

"You had better leave," the cat said.

"I can't!" Alice was backing away from the moonlight.

The torches were coming, closer and closer. At the head of them shone Fá Prongs herself, wrathful and deadly.

"Alice." Petrova caught the small cow's eyes. "Alice, I believe in you. You can do this. Alice, you can jump over the Moon!"

It was said that that night, cows all over Cowland saw a remarkably clear figure of a cow, leaping over the far-away Moon. But that was not all. Beside her flew a dog, a tiny dog with curly brown fur. They were both together in flight.

They landed in Alice's parents' pasture. Her mother was there, gazing at her, delight illuminating her face. "Alice! You've come home!" she cried. "Oh, I'm sorry I ever discouraged you like that! I should've known you could do it!" She ran to Alice and embraced her, tears running down her face.

"It's all right, Mother," said Alice, trying to smile at her canine companion, who was laughing with joy, and hug her mother at the same time. "I forgive you."

Hey diddle, diddle,
The cat played the fiddle,
The cow jumped over the Moon,
The little dog laughed to see such sport,
And the dish ran away with the spoon.

About the Author

Lorna Garlets is a homeschooler who lives in Kalamazoo along with her five younger siblings. Ever since she was seven, she has wanted to be a great author. She has been published in *Unlocked,* a devotional for teens, and writes a monthly newsletter for her family. She is fourteen years old.

Youth Judges' Choice Winner

Safe
Liliana Harkema

I was in the Garden when they came.

I was staring in awe at the summer landscape spread out before me. The flowers bloomed in a million colors through the green-clad valleys and hills, and the air was warm, with a cool breeze that made my two golden braids flutter. I was so lost in the majesty of it all that I didn't hear the footsteps coming toward our cottage until they were just at the bottom of the hill my house and I sat atop.

My heart instantly began to pound, and I could feel myself starting to sweat. *It's them,* I thought. *But no, it couldn't be. They have no reason to come.* They didn't seem to need a reason anymore. *You have nothing to hide.* I thought so, but I had heard a lot of late-night whispers from Mother and Father lately, and it made me suspicious. Then again, it might not be them. It might not be the Nazis at all. *But what if it was?* I needed to tell Mother. I took a deep breath to calm my rapidly beating heart and ran for the cottage.

"Mother, someone's coming!" I cried. Mother emerged from the bedroom with a sleepy Karl in her arms. Mother's mouth was a solemn line, but she didn't seem too anxious.

"Thank you for telling me, Birgit," she said calmly. "I will be outside for a moment. Will you take Karl?"

"But Mother," I pleaded as I set the yawning one-year-old on my hip, "can't I come?" Mother paused for a moment, thinking. It was just a few seconds, but it felt like an hour as I stared around the room at the white walls.

Across from me was the china cabinet. It was built into the wall, and it held some of my family's greatest treasures. My favorite was the little cream pitcher painted with the flowering hills of Austria, my home.

Finally, Mother decided. "You may come." She said softly, "But you must keep Karl." And heaving a sigh, she opened the sky-blue door. As we stepped out into the summer morning, two people came over the hill, and one seemed to be a girl no older than I was (I was twelve). To think my heart was pounding!

But why were they here? I kept on my guard. They could be spies, or Nazis in disguise, or . . . something worse. The girl was with an older woman, who had a red nose and identical expression to Mother. The girl's face was pale and almost gray, and her expression held a slight sadness I thought must go down much farther than her face. It wasn't just her face that was gray. Among all of Austria's summer splendor she looked as dreary as a textbook in the rain. Her clothes were shabby and frayed, her arms and legs skinny and pale, and her long hair limp and tangled.

"Good morning," My Mother called. "I trust your journey went well?"

"About as well as can be expected." The old lady wheezed.

She must have a cold, I thought. Karl squirmed in my arms.

The old lady spoke again. "Well, here she is. Her ship leaves on the first of August, and she has the tickets. I must be going now, but I trust you will care for her well. Be careful, and good luck, young lady. And the woman was gone, coughing all the way down the hill.

I, meanwhile, was bursting with questions. But I supposed I would have to wait because Mother was already talking to the girl.

"My name is Lena, and this is my daughter Birgit, and my son, Karl. I hope you will be very happy here, but before we talk about anything else you must have a nice warm bath. I will run the water for you now, just come this way."

The girl's lips curled upward a little at the mention of warm bath, and she followed Mother into the cottage. Mother ran the bathwater and gave the girl soap and a towel, and finally came back to the kitchen where I was waiting.

"Who is that girl?" I asked instantly. "Why is she here? How long will she stay? Who was that woman? Does Father know?" I paused to take a breath, and Mother interrupted.

"I know you have a lot of questions, my darling, but please let me answer them now." Her voice was patient, and I obeyed. "The girl is Jewish."

My mouth dropped open, and my eyes went wide. "Jewish?" I almost shrieked. "But-but the Nazis! She's in trouble!"

"Hush." My Mother said, "Let me explain. She lived in Germany, in hiding with her parents. However, the Nazis eventually found them. She escaped, but her parents..."

"Oh, Mother, how dreadful." My freckled cheeks burned as I remembered some of the things I had thought about her.

"I know, darling. She fled to a nearby family her parents trusted, and they took care of her for a while and bought her a boat ticket to America under a false identity.

"Why America?" I asked.

"She has some relatives there, and they will take her in."

"But why is she at our house?"

"The family she stayed with are old friends of your Father and I, and they wrote us a letter a few weeks ago, asking if we could take her in. They are leaving the country themselves, but did not have an extra ticket. Your Father and I talked it over, and decided we would take the girl until she can leave for America."

Today was June fifteenth, which meant that girl would be staying for a month and a half! "But who was that woman?"

"A friend of the family the girl stayed with. She very kindly agreed to bring the poor child to us. Does that answer all your questions?"

"Almost." I replied. "But I have two more. Why didn't you tell me about this before?"

"Because" Mother answered, "we wanted to keep you safe. The less you knew, the less you could give away or be questioned about. You must understand that we are responsible for this girl's life. We *cannot* give her away no matter what happens, or she could be killed. Do you understand me, Birgit?"

"Yes, Mother." I said, nodding. "I understand."

"Now, I believe you have one more question for me?" Mother said, heaving a sigh.

"Yes. What is her name?"

"That, I do not know. Her name was not in the letter to protect her if it was intercepted. We will ask her when she has finished her bath."

I nodded, and Mother walked away.

I may have been quiet on the outside, but inside, my mind was racing with all the information. A Jewish orphan was going to hide with us for a month and a half, we had to protect her at all costs, and we didn't even know her name.

I stood up from the hard wooden chair and stared up the stairs. My feet were carrying me, I didn't tell them what to do. *Creak, creak, creak.* The stairs were loud, but the questions in my head were louder. Where would this girl sleep? Where would she eat? We had no spare room.

Now I was in my room. I looked around at it all, wondering if the girl would have to share it. The bed was small, with a faded pink quilt and thick white pillow. Next to the bed I had one window, and it looked out on the hills and valleys of Austria, those same hills and valleys I had been looking at just a few minutes ago, though it could have been days.

My world had turned topsy-turvy in such a brief time, and everything was different. My very *life* was different. I was in danger now.

Beneath the window, in the corner, was my favorite part of the tiny room. A window seat with a soft cotton cushion. It was a perfect space for dreaming, writing, reading, thinking, *anything,* really. I sat down on the cushion.

Across from me was a small set of drawers and hooks above it. Hanging on one of the hooks was my favorite dress, a cream-colored cotton thing with tiny flowers in a rainbow of colors. Next to the chest of drawers was a tiny bookshelf. I only had a few books, but to me they were as precious as diamonds. I had a secret, too. Underneath the cushion, there was a trap door that opened into the inside of the window seat. The compartment was the size of the window seat itself, and if I ever had something to hide, I would put it in there. I've never seen anything like it before.

My brain churned all the information like butter, but I couldn't get my thoughts to solidify. Everything that Mother had just told me swirled and swirled through my head. Mother said that the girl escaped from the nazis. How? Had her parents hidden her, then faced the nazis? Why did she look so ragged? One thing Mother had said grew clearer and clearer in my head. *We are responsible for this girl's life.* We are in danger. But no one would come. Nobody knew. Except for us and the frowning lady. And her, of course. While the thought-milk buttered my brain, I decided one thing. This girl had no friends in the world, not even parents. I was going to change that.

One Month Later

We were in the garden when they came.

We were lying on our backs in the soft grass, the sun going down behind us, and we were talking. Anneliese -yes, that was her name- had not talked at all at first, except for the occasional "Yes, ma'am." or "No, sir." But little by little she talked about things. Never about her life since her parents' death, but about the life she had lived before, as she put it, "The nazis came, *heil*-ing Hitler and chasing Jews." Instead she talked of the places she had visited, the books she had read, and the friends she had made.

Today she was telling me about a trip to Paris, her eyes glowing as she spoke. Her hair was now recognizable as a rich, nutty brown, and she was less skinny, though her eyes still held that deep, painful sadness, even behind the glow. She stopped talking abruptly.

"I hear footsteps." She whispered. The glow had left her eyes, which had become wide in fear. My heart began to pound, just like it had a month ago. That had been a good surprise, but the reason for this visitor was unknown.I was sweating.

"We should tell Mother and Father." I said firmly, trying to keep my voice steady. And so we ran inside. Mother and Father were at the table, laughing about some joke or another.

"Someone's coming!" I cried. Mother and Father stopped laughing immediately, and their faces became grave. Clearly, they were not expecting someone tonight. My Father grabbed his binoculars, his most prized possession, and ran outside. He returned shortly, and his face was pale. "Lena, it's *them.*"

"Oh, Lennart!" Mother's face turned pale, too. I was confused, and I could tell by Anneliese's expression that she was, too.

"What will we do with her?" Mother asked, her voice shaking.

"Hide her," Father replied, "But where..."

Suddenly, I understood. The Nazis were coming.

And now we *did* have something to hide. But we didn't have a place to hide her. I mentally walked through every room of my home, searching for a spot. The footsteps were getting closer every second, I knew, and we were running out of time. I knew a spot.

"The window seat!" I blurted out, making everyone jump. "The hollow seat!" Father nodded, and I grabbed Anneliese's hand and raced up the stairs. She didn't know what I was talking about, I had never shown her the compartment. We ran into my room, where I lifted the cushion and flung open the trapdoor. Anneliese's mouth opened into a wide "O".

"Get inside!" I said frantically, and she obeyed. "Don't make a sound. We'll get you when the coast is clear. I promise." Someone was coming upstairs.

"Thank you." She squeaked. "I won't."

I shut the trapdoor.

It was only Mother upstairs, grabbing an unhappy Karl from his bed. She handed him to me, and I held onto him tightly. I wished I was one year old, blissfully unaware of the war.

"Oo-ba?" he asked, confused.

"It's alright, Karl, be quiet now." I comforted.

I heard voices downstairs. I flew down the steps with Mother close behind, and in the doorway, I saw two officers talking to Father. They informed us in harsh voices that they had heard a rumor of an escaped Jew in our house. What rumor? From whom?

"There is no Jew in our house." Father said calmly. "Unless he or she is living under our beds, I have no reason to think we are a household of more than four." He smiled faintly, but the soldiers were as grave as a tombstone.

They said they would search anyway, and Father let them. Why? Couldn't he refuse? These questions ran through my head, while deep in my heart I knew that he couldn't refuse. It would mean danger and suspicion, and it wouldn't stop them from searching.

The soldiers left the entryway, stomping through the house, while my family stayed put. Karl became heavier and heavier in my arms as we heard cupboards banging shut and things crashing. Once I heard what had to be the tinkle of breaking china, and Mother gasped.

Several minutes passed, and finally the soldiers came back. Karl whimpered. Now they were heading upstairs, and my breathing grew heavier. What if Anneliese coughed? What if they looked under the cushion? What would they do to her if she was found? It couldn't happen. No. It just couldn't.

Drawers were being opened and shut upstairs, boots stomping from room to room.

I waited.

And waited.

And waited.

It felt like a day. A month. A year.

The soldiers came downstairs. They looked angry and left without saying a word, slamming the door behind them. Still, none of us moved. Even Karl was silent. I started to step forwards, but Father put up his hand to stop me.

So we waited longer.

Slowly, Father moved forwards, took the binoculars from the shelf where they lay, and walked outside. I suppose he thought they could still be hiding somewhere, waiting for us to bring Anneliese out.

A few minutes later he came back through the door, smiled and said, "It's all clear."

I let out a breath of relief that I hadn't realized I'd been holding in. I handed Karl to Mother and tore up the stairs, through the hallway and into my bedroom.

I tossed the window seat cushion away, and there was Anneliese, looking small and scared.

"You're safe!" I shouted. "*You're safe!*" those words were like the sweetest song I'd ever heard. I helped her out of the window seat, and together we ran down the stairs to Mother and Father.

I don't know quite how it happened, but suddenly we were all hugging and crying and laughing. Anneliese, who had gone through so much and never shed a single tear over it, had tears streaming down her cheeks.

"Ann-lee! Ann-lee!" Karl cried in his baby gibberish. But wait. He was saying it over and over again. It *wasn't* baby gibberish.

"Shhh, everyone, listen!" I hushed.

"Oh!" Cried Mother, "He's saying *Anneliese!* He's said his first word!" And everyone was crying and laughing and hugging some more.

I had no idea what was to come, but at that very moment we were safe, and that was all that mattered.

About the Author

Liliana Harkema is an avid reader and writer who loves books of all genres, but especially historical fiction. She also dances, reads, sews, reads, bakes, reads, dances and reads a little, too. She lives in Grand Rapids with her mom and dad, sister, 11 crazy chickens, two rambunctious cats and one snuggly rabbit.

Youth Judges' Choice Runner-Up

Is this real?
Frank Yanover

Chapter One: Signals.

They are coming. I can sense it. I can sense their malevolent disturbance, an irrational mistake that shouldn't be here. It is them. I can tell. The Kralitak, alien worms. They are getting closer.

Suddenly, it lurches into view, looking real but somehow fake. It is in the body of my mother, smiling with her face. It cackles, opening her mouth so far the jawbone simply breaks off and dangles limply. Reaching its hands toward her head, it twists it completely upside down. Her neck snaps sickeningly. Blood gushes forth but her head stays on, only adding to the horror. She drops to one knee. Backing up, I bang my head onto the wall behind me. I suddenly feel dizzy and collapse to the floor, cornered. The Kralitak lunges out of her forehead, leaving a small, circular hole. It flies through the air, emanating the stench of brimstone. As it strikes me, my dream ends.

Chapter Two: What really happened?

I wake up screaming to find my parents in the room. "Honey? Are you okay? Did you have a nightmare?" my mother asks. "Yes, a worm was att-" I begin explaining when I notice she has a bandage on her forehead. The hairs on the back of my neck stand up. Goosebumps form on my head and arms. "I fell off a cliff. In my dream." I stammer. She clearly doesn't believe me, but doesn't press. "Yep. Just a little fall." I repeat. Her eyes are a little cloudy, and her speech is haphazard, as though her mouth doesn't work quite right. Her head is lolling about five degrees to the left, not quite enough to notice unless you deliberately look. Was it real? No, just a subconscious hallucination or even a coincidence. "Better be careful. Those nightmares can be dangerous." She says, closing the door behind her.

Alien worms? No way it was real. Those thoughts are comforting, but they cannot completely quell the dark thoughts rising in my mind. This time, I slowly drift into unconsciousness with no night terrors.

My alarm goes off at seven. When I wake up, I head downstairs for breakfast. My parents are cooking eggs, and I apologize for my nightmare. "What nightmare?" my father asks. "Uhhh...the one I woke you up screaming with. The wor-falling nightmare." I respond casually, though my mind is racing. "You didn't wake us up," my father remarks skeptically. What? I look at my mother in confusion, and she comments, "You must have dreamed you had a nightmare." They get a good laugh at that as my frustration grows. My mom's bandage is gone, and she speaks and moves her head normally. What the--?

On the drive to school, I am so deeply engrossed in my book that I barely notice what is happening. She drops me off, and I leave without a word until I notice this isn't my school. I am in a courtyard. She gets out and smiles viciously. With her hands at her side, her head seemingly rotates of its own accord until it is upside down. The monstrosity moves toward me. "Mom," I exclaim, "Is that supposed to be you?"

She snarls and drops to the ground. A writhing worm bursts from her forehead. It slithers toward me and I am almost supernaturally paralyzed by fear. It connects with my flesh and rears back to strike, like a cobra, then jams its toothy maw through my skin. Horrified, I can only watch. I feel another presence in my skull and in my mind, another voice. "Ssubmit to the Kralitak. **Sssubmit to the Kralitak. SSSSUBMIT TO THE KRALITAK!**" it hisses. Its compulsion is too strong, so I can no longer resist. I obey. **"KILL!"** it hisses, louder this time, **"KILL!"**

Chapter Three: Could this be it?

My head snaps back and I awaken to find a crowd of children around me. "Robert fainted. Robert fainted. Robert fainted." they say, pointing at me and laughing. I groggily sit up and move to kill them when I realize the Kralitak isn't in control anymore. It is me. "The Kralitak is coming! Run!" I yell. "The what now? The 'crab attack?' Yeah no. He's delusional." one says. What is going on? Is this real? Is that real? Is nothing real? A sense of fear and loss of control comes over me. "Get up. You fainted in math class. Mr. Dolvel is not happy," another says, roughly pulling me to my feet. He has a small hole in his forehead. No. I quickly scramble away from him. Another steps coldly over me, her forehead hole glistening with blood. I get to my feet quickly and run, but as I look back, I notice they all have holes in their foreheads. In unison, all heads slowly but surely turn upside down and their jaws fall off. Teeth lengthen and appear in many widening gashes through their faces. Blood seeps from their countless injuries and pools. The pool grows wider and wider. **"Ssubmit to the Kralitak. Sssubmit to the Kralitak. SSSSUBMIT TO THE KRALITAK!"**

they all chant. The rapidly expanding bloody pool catches up to me and I slip down into it, sinking farther and farther. I could not possibly get up to the surface in time, even if I could move my muscles. Eventually, I must inhale a mouthful of blood and I choke. I keep sinking, deeper and deeper, into the deep maroon of unconsciousness.

Chapter Four: This can't be right.

I wake up back in my bed. Is this heaven? No, I am still trapped in the ever-deepening pits of illusions, mirrors, falsehoods, and hallucinations. I don't even know what the hallucinations are anymore. These thoughts are far too deep for the morning.

I leap out of bed, take a deep breath, and walk upstairs to get breakfast. Upstairs? No, downstairs was only a dream. This time – not this time, there never was a first time – my father is making pancakes. It was only a dream. Only a dream. He turns toward me, and his eyes narrow in suspicion. "Why is there dried blood on your face?" he queries.

I open my mouth to speak but see the small hole in his forehead, seeping blood. No bandage. I quickly say the first thing that comes into my head, "Just a little ketchup from dinner. Yesterday's dinner." "We didn't have ketchup with dinner, silly. It isn't even in our fridge. If you keep lying, I just might have to appropriately discipline you." After saying this, he smiles with many, too many, hypnotizing white teeth. Not completely white – they are speckled with red. "I don't know why my face is ketchupy," I respond. With glee, he cackles, "Bad boys deserve punishment."

Maniacal laughter ensues. He steps slowly toward me. "Father, no!" I plead. He shoves me to the ground and grabs a kitchen knife. "Bad boys deserve punishment," he repeats. His eyes grow cloudy. I am in a corner. "Bad boys deserve punishment," he says with conviction as he swings the heavy blade at my face. I watch in anticipatory horror as the blade approaches me, so sharp I can barely see it. It connects and waves of crimson splay from my face. I fall to my knees in pure agony. "More punishment has become necessary," he monotones. He swings it again and I know I am finished. The blade connects with my chest. The last thing I feel is searing pain.

Chapter Five: Or can it?

I open my eyes to find myself floating on a raft in the middle of a bloody sea. I will not even question this, and only deal with the now and not the was. Oh. Someone must have rescued me when I was drowning.

"Help," I yell, "Help." No one can hear me, I realize with despair.

All of sudden, my raft jolts upward about an inch. It repeats, stronger this time. What is going on? I roll over and look down to see what looks like water snakes, hundreds of them. They back up, then slam into the raft. They are Kralitak worms. No. They collide into the raft with the force of an elephant. It splinters and I fall into the maroon ocean, into the waiting mouths of over 500 Kralitak. **"SSSSUBMIT TO THE KRALIT-"** I scream, then my mouth fills with terrible metallic blood.

Chapter Six: Truth ... or is it?

I awaken, gasping, in the school nurse's office. One lady is there. "Hi," she introduces, "You tripped and scratched your forehead." I feel, and sure enough, there is a bandage on my forehead. "Would you like a soda?" She asks. "Sure," I answer. "Do you have a Coke?" "Sure," she responds, and hands me a large soda in a cup, with a long straw. I take it and sip eagerly. Something is wrong. The Coke tastes strangely metallic.

I pop the lid off, and the "Coke" is deep red. I look up at the nurse, but she has disappeared. The straw morphs into a long, vile worm while I sip. It crawls into my mouth. I can feel it squirm. It pops through the roof of my mouth, into my brain. The last thing I hear before everything goes dark is **"SSSSUBMIT TO THE KRALITAK!"**

Chapter Seven: Spoiler Alert: It isn't

I am floating alone in a dark void. Cold nothingness envelopes me. If I am dead, this must be hell. What did I do? Three days ago I was rude to my mother. Last Sunday I skipped church to play video games. Maybe I said OMG one too many times.

I don't even know how long I have been floating. Has it been hours, days, or even years? I am so hungry. When will this madness end? A body floats into view. My mother.

Oh, I am so hungry. She opens her mouth as if to speak, but no words come out. She looks so delicious. I need food. I am unable to resist. When she comes near, I move as if to hug her, then bite her neck.

She tastes so tender and filling that I barely notice her final expression of repulsive terror. Mmmm. I eat her arms, head, and neck but save the rest for later. It is only minutes before I realize the true horror of what I have done. I just murdered my mother and engaged in cannibalism. How could I? I push her so far away that I can never reach her again. Eventually, I starve, floating in the eternal zero gravity abyss.

Chapter Eight: Sadness

I wake up to find my father tapping me and crying. "Robert, wake up," he weeps, "Your mother died." "No!" I scream, "What happened?" "They found what was left of her in a ditch. Her head and arms were missing, and one human tooth was found in the bite marks. She was cannibalised," he says grimly. "Oh no!" I respond.

With trepidation, I check inside my mouth to find one incisor is missing. It was real. I actually ate my mother.

A week later, I go to her funeral. I stand in front of the coffin to make my regards, crying. Her body jolts upright. Blood drips from her missing head and splatters upon the ground. She moves closer and closer. A voice seems to come from within me, saying "Give me back my head. Give me back my head. **GIVE ME BACK MY HEAD!**" Something moves inside my stomach.

I look down and can see inside my chest. Teeth are gnawing at me. The remnants of my last meal, disgusting stomach acids, and my mothers head and arms spill from me. A gaping hole, about 8 inches wide and long, is carved from my belly. Her severed arms pick up her head and place it upon her kneeling body. They then attach themselves. Somehow, they stay on. Her expression of repulsive terror remains. I collapse to the ground, unable to breathe. Oh, the irony. She laughs as I die.

Chapter Nine: Dreams

I awaken, like so many times in the past week, but this time it feels different. More real somehow. Was it all a dream? Maybe. Maybe not.

I head across the hall for breakfast. Both my parents are there. "Mom! I'm so glad you're okay!" I exclaim. "Why wouldn't I be okay?" she asks, puzzled. Ignoring the remark, I hug her.

My hands sink through her like vapor and she slowly dissipates.

Looking over, I realize dad is gone too. "No!" I scream. **"YESSSS"** voices from within, Kralitak voices, respond.

It bursts from my forehead. My last thought before I submit to its malicious will is, "How long has it been there?"

Chapter Ten: Insights
Is this real?
For how long?
I don't believe you.
Stop the lies.
They are lies.

Oh yes.
It doesn't lie.
Of course not.
Why would it?
It has no need to.
With me, no need.
I can do anything.
I would rather be a servant
in the house of Lies
than dwell in the tents
of Truth.
Malsalms 84:10
Consider this:
Is this more lies than truth?
~~~or~~~
Is this more truth than lies?
I hope you questioned more than just this.

About the Author

Frank Yanover is the Write Michigan 2024-2025 Judges' Choice Runner-Up winner in the Youth Category.

Youth Readers' Choice Winner

The Pirate Cove's Treasure
Addison Craig

The rumbling bus pulls up to the old rotten sign that says, "Camp Pirate's Cove." You might think this is a camp that teaches kids how to be pirates, but this is a summer camp where kids hang out with their friends and eat s'mores. I have been looking forward to coming back since I left last summer. I miss my friend Annie and her spooky stories. Annie is a very outgoing person. I also miss my intelligent friend Maggie and her love for books. She definitely keeps me in check.

I grab my bag and step off the bus. The Camp Leader, Ms. Gray tells us to line up in single file so we know what cabin we will be in. When I get to the front of the line I see the sadness and red blotches on Ms. Gray's face, which is weird because she always has a big grin. She forces a smile and croaks "It's nice to see you again, Abby."

"Nice to see you too," I say back.

"Ok… You are in cabin 4 this summer," Ms. Gray points down at a map. "Don't forget to come to the campfire after you put your stuff in your cabin."

I walk into the cabin and see the old wooden bed frames with a gray mattress. I grab my flower printed sheets and stretch it across the mattress. I place my overnight bag on the bed and the old springs make a weird sound. I also see Annie sleeping. Her snores are as loud as an engine. I walk on the floors that creak when you take every step but Annie sleeps through the noise. I grab her shoulder and shake her.

"Mom, just five more minutes," she grumbles.

"It's Abby," I whisper. She opens her eyes as wide as she possibly can. She jumps onto me and knocks me over. I slam down hard on the ground and groan. She pops up. "I missed you a lot and I… I," she tears up a little bit.

"I missed you too," I say softly. I give her a *normal* hug.

She sniffs, "What time is it?"

"Um… almost noon," I replied. We hear the old door creak open and see Maggie with her face burried in a book. Maggie looks up and gives us her geniune smile, and our group is complete.

"What's in there?" I ask as I point to her bulging bag.

"My books," Maggie answers.

I grab the handles and drag the bag, which feels like a hundred pounds, across the floor.

Maggie, Annie, and I sit on the stump by the campfire. Ms. Gray shakes as she stands in front of the campers. She wrings her hands.

"I have some unfortunate news to share. The camp is closing, due to some unforeseen financial hardships, so let's do our best to make it a great summer," Ms. Gray announces.

What, this is so unfair! This is my home away from home. I spent most of my summers here. I start biting my nails. Everyone is in disbelief. I feel a tear slowly fall down my face.

When we get back to the cabin we just sit in silence. You could hear a pin drop.

Bang! The cabin shakes from the loud thunder. It's late and Maggie and I are sitting on Annie's bed while she is telling us another spooky story.

"The founder of the camp sailed all the seas and landed on Camp Pirate's Cove. He buried all his treasure on this land but no one knows where the hidden treasure is located." Annie is known for telling elaborate stories with such enthusiasm you would think they were real.

"This is just one of your fake stories. I want to read my book." Maggie says with an annoyed look on her face.

"Not true!" Annie protests."As I was saying, one night a group of Pirate's Cove campers went on a search to find the treasure. Sadly, they never found it and those campers were never found." Lighting strikes just on cue. "All that is left of those campers is their story."

"I still think that story is fake," Maggie says unconvinced.

"We can give Annie the benefit of the doubt," I say.

"You don't believe me," Annie says, staring us in the eyes.

Maggie and I nod.

"Well... I still want to find that treasure," Annie says.

"First, where do we start?" I ask, listing off on my fingers, "Second, what will we do with the money?"

"I think I have a lead. Lately, I've been working out a plan and there is an old map in the cafeteria that could lead to the treasure." Annie answers. "I saw the map when I was getting lunch yesterday. We could get a mansion and a water slide."

"You can't just go outside during a storm!" Maggie says disapproving the idea.

This sounded like an exciting adventure and just what we needed to make this was our best summer together at Camp Pirate's Cove. "The storm is miles away, and it stopped raining. Come on, it will be fun." I say enthusiastically thinking of what Ms. Gray said a few days ago.

"I still want to buy a mansion and get a water slide," Annie says dreamily. "What's the worst that could happen?"

"We could get lost, we could lose our free time privileges, and worst, die!" Maggie lists off.

I pick up Maggie like a baby.

"Put me down," she hisses, "At least let me grab my flashlight."

We look out the window to see if there's anyone around.

"Follow me," Annie says. We follow Annie to the cafeteria just to find out that it is locked.

"Let's just go back to the cabin before we get caught," Maggie whispers.

"Wait... I have a bobby pin," Annie yanks it out of her hair.

"Are you sure that is going to work?" I say questioning, "That only works in movies."

"It's all we got," Annie says reassuringly. *Maggie is probably rolling her eyes right now.*

Click!

"Aha!"

"Shhhhh, we don't want to be caught," says Maggie.

Annie opens the door, and we walk in the cafeteria.

Logic overtakes me and I ask, "Wait, aren't there cameras?"

"I disabled the cameras at lunch," Annie said.

We creep on the tile floor. The tiles are so cold I think my hands and knees are going to get frostbite. Annie leads us to the map in a picture frame that hangs in the kitchen. We open the swing door that leads to the kitchen.

"Be very careful," Annie says slowly, "We don't want to wake up the lunch lady."

I slip on a substance and accidentally run into Maggie. She falls on Annie, and goes face first into the mop. The handle of the mop hits the map's picture frame off of the nail while the map goes flying to the floor.

Crash!

"Sorry," My face is red. I get ready for the anger swelling up in Annie and Maggie. Then we all start laughing much louder than the accident that happened moments ago. We hear a door open and stand like we are frozen icicles. Maggie turns off the flashlight, and we creep back out of the kitchen.

"You get back here little raccoons!" The lunch lady yells holding a large wooden spoon and swinging it around like a lasso. "I'll feed you to the children!" She hollers. We get up on our feet and hide under a table.

She starts running in our direction, so we bolt out of the cafeteria into the woods. I lead us farther and farther into the darkness. I hear the crunching of the leaves under my feet. I am the more athletic one in the group, so I easily maintain the lead.

Once I feel we are a safe distance away, I slow my pace to a halt. We are too tired and out of breath to run anymore. We need to hide. I ponder on what to do. "Come on," I whisper. We start climbing the pine tree to our right, going up and up.

In the distance, we see the lunch lady trip over a log as her wooden prosthetic foot goes flying up into the air and lands in the abyss."You can run but you can't hide," she snickers. She grabs a flashlight out of her apron pocket and starts searching for the "raccoons". She lets out a moan, "I guess raccoons can hide."

I want to burst out laughing, but she will hear me. She grabs a big stick and uses it to hobble back to the camp. *In other circumstances I would feel bad for her, but she was chasing us into the woods.* We wait quietly until we can't hear the leaves crunch beneath her foot. We slowly climb down from the tree.

Annie slips on the branch when she is climbing down. "Annie!" I snatch her hand while Maggie grabs her other hand and Annie finds her balance. We find the trail, following it back in the direction of the camp.

"Okay we need to follow the bank of the river and take a right at the boulder. Then take a left," Annie points at the map, "Wait, it's a dead end."

"We just stole an old, useless map and got chased by the lunch lady for nothing!" Maggie stomps with frustration in her voice. "I'm going back to the cabin,"

"Wait, we could still look," Annie proposes.

"There is nothing to look for, your story was fake," Maggie storms off.

"Abby," Annie's eyes tear up.

"Sorry," I say quietly. I walk the long path to the cabin. *I can't believe that the camp is closing. It was my dream to someday be a counselor.* I start crying, unsure what to do next. *I don't want Maggie to see me like this.* I look up at the stars that look like little lights in the sky to hide my emotion. One of the many reasons why I love Camp Pirate's Cove so much. I just gaze into the sky, and spot the Little Dipper and the Big Dipper. *I wish I could do something about camp.* My thoughts got interrupted by someone running at me. *Oh no, the lunch lady found me!* I quickly turn to see Annie running up to me.

"Abby, Maggie, where are you?" Annie loudly whispers.

"I'm right here," I mumble, "I thought you were finding *treasure.*"

"The map was folded in a way that it was hiding the location of the treasure," she unfolds it, "See."

"Let's go get Maggie!"

The three of us run in unison with hope that we will find the treasure. We sprint the winding path that the map told us to go on. The spot leads us rigt to Ms. Gray's cabin and I am flabbergasted.

"That can't be right. We probably took a wrong turn somewhere," Maggie says.

"I want to see what's inside," Annie says, starting to walk into the cabin.

"Let's go, we are this close to maybe finding something," I say. I grab Maggie's wrist, so she will follow us into the cabin.

"We're asking to get caught," Maggie mumbles. "I am not going to get blamed for this."

I agree with Maggie, but we could get a thousand or possibly a million dollars. We slowly tip-toe through the cabin and see Ms. Gray is sleeping on her side with her mouth open. We find the stairs that go to a basement, assuming the treasure would be underground. As we move down the stairs, I can hear that there is a leak in the ceiling. Maggie's flashlight makes the basement glow up. We decide it is best to split up to search for the treasure in what seems to be endless junk. I spot an old photograph of the founder standing in front of Ms. Gray's cabin; the very same cabin that we are in now. Before I can say anything the floor gives out and I let out a yelp. Annie and Maggie rush over to my aid and drag me out of the hole I have fallen into. Annie looks into the hole, "Guys what is that?"

"That's... that's a treasure chest!" Maggie jumps for joy.

Just as we were about to celebrate, Ms. Gray runs down the stairs, "Girls!" She yells with a confused look on her face. Maggie looks like she saw a ghost and Annie is trying to pull out the chest.

"What's going on here?" She says sternly.

Where do I start?

"We were looking for a treasure and it led here so we started searching in your cabin." Annie confesses.

"And my leg fell through the floor," I say.

"Yeah, these floors are too dangerous to walk on." Ms. Gray says.

"We are deeply sorry, but are we in trouble?" Maggie asks.

"This is just a lot to take in," Ms. Gray answers, "I always thought that the story was a myth."

"I told you there was treasure," Annie looks at Maggie with a smugly smile on her face.

"Who would have thought that old map was the key to the founder's treasure." Ms. Gray declares.

We are all so excited that no one notices blood running down my leg and soaking my Nike sock.

"Let's get Abby to the nurse," Ms. Gray says in a motherly tone as she examines my wound.

We walk through the cafeteria and the lunch lady is glaring at me in anger. *Does she know it was us that she was chasing earlier tonight?* She probably connected the dots already while she is mopping up our mess. Annie, Maggie, and I let out a chuckle while we head into the nurse's office who asks, "What happened?"

"I might have fallen through a floor," I say.

"Annie, Maggie go to bed. We'll address this in the morning," Ms. Gray says with care, recognizing that the story of our great adventure would have to wait.

"We hope your leg feels better," Annie and Maggie say together.

"Night," I wave goodbye.

The nurse tends my wounds. It is really painful. I finally realize how tired I am and drift off to sleep.

The sun shines in my eyes. My leg hurts when I walk but I want to go and find my friends. There are not a lot of people awake right now. When I walk into the cabin Maggie is reading one of her books and Annie is sleeping. Maggie looks up from her book.

"How is your leg?" She asks.

"It's been better," I answer, "Where's the treasure?"

"When Annie wakes up we will discuss it," she explains.

"I also can't believe this is the last time we will be at Camp Pirate's Cove," I say with a lump in my throat.

"Same," Maggie agrees.

"Good morning," Annie says with a yawn.

"Let's get ready, so we can head over to Ms. Gray's cabin," Maggie suggests.

I throw on shorts and a t-shirt. We head out the door. Ms. Gray greets us as we walk in.

"Good morning girls, thank you for coming. I wanted to talk about the gold you found. This is an amazing find and it is about twenty thousand dollars worth."

I thought it would be a million dollars, but it is still a lot of money.

"I was talking to all of your parents about it and they said it was up to you girls to decide what to do with the money," Ms. Gray definitely is still surprised about the whole thing.

"May we have a moment to discuss?" Maggie asks.

"Of course," Ms. Gray smiles.

We sit at the table while Ms. Gray leaves the cabin.

"I don't think we can afford a mansion," Annie confirms.

"So what will we do with all the money?" Maggie asks.

"We could split it three ways," I suggest. Then an idea pops into my mind "Or we could donate it to the camp!"

"That's a great idea!" Maggie says, "Then the camp won't close!"

"Let's do that," Annie agrees.

We go tell Ms. Gray.

"Girls, that is so sweet, but it is unnecessary," she tells us.

"We want to," Annie, Maggie, and I say in sync.

"Are you sure you want to do this?" Ms. Gray asks.

"Yes," we say.

Ms. Gray steps in front of all the campers in the cafeteria and announces, "I know everyone is upset about the camp closing, but Abby, Annie, and Maggie have some good news to tell you."

We confidently walk in front of the campers.

"I know you are all aware of the legend about our founding father and how he buried treasure on this land," Annie says.

"Last night, we found the treasure that was buried in secret and it is worth twenty thousand dollars," adds Maggie.

"And we all love the camp, it's where we spend summer together. We were devastated that it is closing, so we are donating it to the camp. Which means CAMP IS NOT CLOSING!" I proclaim loudly. Everyone stands up and claps, even the old lunch lady.

The familiar sounds of Camp Pirate's Cove surround me as I slowly open my eyes. I get my daily coffee and go stand outside remarking on the familiarity and beauty of this place, I now call home. I see children playing and giggling like I used to when I was a camper. I smile. *What would have happened if the camp had closed that one summer?* I ponder this question for a while, but know, fate had better plans.

About the Author

Addison Craig, age 12, is an avid reader with a particular fondness for the *Percy Jackson* series. She enjoys learning and loves spending time at the beach, especially searching for seashells and swimming in the ocean. When she's not lost in a good book or enjoying the sun and sand, Addi can be found spending time with her big sister, family, friends and her dog, Lola. A competitive soccer player, she brings the same energy and focus to the field as she does to her studies and hobbies. Addi enjoys helping others and always appreciates the company of a great book.

Youth Published Finalist

Suicide Hotline, Make The Call
Frances Heethuis

As I walk to school, the sun cast across my face, I am finally happy.

Everything is good. I have my best friend, my dad, it's the last day of school; life is good. There's something so special about walking in a small town in Maine. While I open the heavy wood door, I can't wait to sign yearbooks, and close that same heavy door behind me. I walk through the musty halls, and dance in the fact that it's the last time. Walking into the class, I greet my teacher.

"Hey Mr. Tinker! Last day!" I say.

"Yep! What are your summer plans?" He asks. My lips form the biggest grin.

"I'm going to Hawaii with Eleanor and my dad!" I responded excitedly. He nods, and I walk slowly to my seat in the back of the class. I grab my journal and write:

> Aurelia Ling   June 6th, 2024
> Hey! I just got to school, and I checked in with Eleanor - my best friend. We're gonna spend the WHOLE summer together! I feel bad for Ellie. She's so excited for summer so she can escape all of the people who have been mean to her this year. Everyone makes fun of her for the color of her skin, but she's my favorite person in the WORLD so... the bell just rang, I gotta go! Bye Diary!

My first 3 classes are the worst— math, Spanish, then PE. But as I walk to lunch, I get so excited I almost start skipping. The crowded lunchroom smells like teen spirit if you ask me, but I'll miss it. Something is off... where's Ellie? If she's not in our normal spot, she must be outside. I mean, it's a pretty nice day! I walked out, and the automatic doors shut behind me. I saw Derek, Leiaa, and Maisee, but no Eleanor. As I left the shade of the building and went into the bright sun, I heard ringing.

"If they don't pick up on the second ring, I'M GONNA JUMP!!" I hear a voice scream. It isn't just a voice though, it was... Eleanor.

"NO!" I yelled, as I ran ahead to look up at her. Eleanor is on the roof, and she wants to jump. Tears start streaming down my face, and I continue to scream. "Ellie NO. Don't do it. You don't have to go to this stupid school anymore, we can both go somewhere where everyone is smart, and they love you for who you are. I can't process it, I'm just empty. Ellie starts to cry, and I can't bear myself. She never said anything about, well, anything like this! I need to get her down.

"Just… don't try to catch me." Ellie says. I don't know what that means. 'Don't try to'--- she's gonna jump. Eleanor throws herself off the roof, and I scream. All I can hear is the phone answering.

"Stay calm." The answerer says. *"This is the suicide hotline, you can tell us anything. We can help. Just stay calm."* I run as fast as I can, feeling the brisk wind take the tears off my face.

"SOMEBODY, ANYBODY, PLEASE, HELP!!!" I scream. All I get in return is blank faces.

"Aurelia, slow down, what's wrong?" Mr. Tinker responds. I start balling, and he holds me tight in an embrace.

"No, stop, no! Go! HELP! I… Eleanor. She jumped off the roof!" I scream. His face changes from confused, to sad, to absolute and complete horror. He runs outside, and it's completely silent. Everyone cleared, and now no one is outside except me, Mr. Tinker, and Eleanor. Mr. Tinker runs to Eleanor and immediately dials a number on his phone. He throws the phone into the grass, and rolls Eleanor over.

"Oh my gosh. Oh my gosh. OH MY GOSH!" Mr. Tinker screeches. All I can see is blood. Scrapes gushing out with so. much. blood. I can't see any rise and fall in her chest, and all I can do is scream and cry. I collapse, getting a few scratches of my own from falling on the concrete.

I must've blacked out. I wake up, and I see officers all around, and Ellie isn't there. I try to sit up, but I'm too weak with grief. I need to find Mr. Tinker, I need to ask if Eleanor is still… I can't finish that thought. I finally muster the strength to get up, and all I can do is stare. The school is empty. The playground is quiet. No one is around, except for me and the officers. I wander slowly to an officer whose name tag says 'Officer Val Richardson'. My voice is still hoarse from screaming and crying as I say,

"Excuse me, officer… Val? Do you know what condition Eleanor Whins is in?"

"I'm really sorry kid," Officer Val starts. "I'm afraid your friend just didn't make it." I choke out a sob, and I don't know what to do with myself. I want to run. I want to run far, far away. I want to run over the low hills with the lush fields of grass, I want to run over the mountains with strenuous terrains, I want to run.

"Thank you for telling me," I say, my voice breaking. Now I will run. I'll run home, run to my room, and cry. Just cry. I'm not even past the building and I see my dad. He's sitting on a bench, crying, waiting for me. He sees me, and immediately gets up to hug me.

"Oh, honey, I'm so sorry." He says. He tries to comfort me, but I just shake. I cry, and cry, and cry. *My best friend* is GONE. She's not coming back.

On the drive home, I look out the window up to the sky. Tears still caressing my face, I wish it was night, so I could count every single glowing star spread across the deep dark blue. As we pull into my driveway, I can't help but think what I would be doing right now if there was no burning tragedy. I would be planning for Hawaii! I would be stuck up in my room, completely oblivious to how bad Eleanor's situation was, and I would plan. What if I had stayed in the moment? What if I had been a better friend? What if I could have helped her? What if it was... my fault? I scream, and the tears burst out full force; almost as if my eyes are a riverbed and my face is the cliff behind a waterfall.

"Dad, it's my fault." I wail, my voice gravelly.

"NO." He says sternly. "Don't go down that path." My dad's voice brings me back to a state of peace, and I can finally calm down at least a little.

"But what if–" I start, as he cuts me off.

"You couldn't do anything. This was bound to happen. If that was how she felt, then she would've jumped anyway. This is not anything about you." He says. I pop open my car door, put in the code for the garage, and burst inside. I grab a bag of chips, –though I'm not even hungry– I grab my laptop, and book it to my bedroom. The yellow walls and the much-too-happy rose caressed curtains are a familiar home to me, but somehow it just makes me feel more out of place. Out of nowhere, I have an impulse, and I scream to my dad,

"We're still going to Hawaii, right?" I feel selfish, insensitive, and I feel like an absolute jerk.

"If you still want to," he starts. "I thought you might not want to since..."

"Closure." I interrupt him. "I need closure. You need closure. We all need..." I say, trailing off.

"I think that's a great idea. Pack your bags, we leave tomorrow." My dad says lovingly.

"Welcome aboard Delta airlines! Have a good flight." The intercom of the airplane says. I'm nervous, I never liked airplanes. My dad squeezes my hand as we take off. I grab my small journal, and start to write.

Aurelia Ling   June, 7th 2024

I can't believe how ignorant I was being. I just read my journal from the day Eleanor died, and I cant stop thinking about what could've been if I was with her instead of writing in a stupid journal. This is my last entry.

I keep feeling Eleanor around me, like she's still here. I know it wasn't my fault, but I still keep thinking of so many ways it WAS my fault. Anyway, I can`t write anymore. Bye diary. Forever.

I try to sleep, hoping I can drift away in the hours from Maine to Hawaii.

"Come again soon, and thank you for flying with Delta!" As I wake up, the light pours into my eyes.

"Already??" I ask my dad. He looks at me and smiles, knowing I am glad to have slept through the whole flight.

"Yes dear," he says, "we're here." I form the biggest grin. While people start to get up to get their stuff out of the crowded overhead bins, I start to feel the excitement fade. There was an empty seat by the window, and it wouldn't be empty if Eleanor was here. I decide to shake it off, I can't let anything get in the way of this trip. It has to be perfect. For Eleanor.

"Ready dad?" I say, trying to change the subject in my brain.

"Yes. First stop, hotel pool!" He answers, with a big smile. I smile back, making sure he can't tell it's forced. While we're leaving the airport, I make up conversations with Eleanor in my head; as if she's here. The whole way to the lobby of the Waikiki Grand Hotel, I imagine Ellie's long, black braids, her beautiful hazel eyes, but most of all; her comfort. I wish she was *here*. Not just here in Hawaii with me, but here. With me, laughing, talking, being. But life is life. This is real.

"CALABUNGA!!" Dad screams as he jumps into the pool. He knew it would embarrass me, but at least my mind is almost completely off of Eleanor. Already wet from the splash, I decide to just jump in. The pool is freezing, but I don't even care. Who knew it would be so warm in Hawaii? The light blue chlorinated water ends abruptly and all you can see past the end of the pool is the big deep blue ocean. I can smell the ocean, and I've already seen 5 groups of dolphins! I couldn't love Hawaii more. Except if… no. I won't go down that path. My dad sees that I look distracted, and he splashes my face with the cold water.

"Dad!" I yell. He grins at me, and I splash him back. "No amount of cold water splashes could ruin my mood. This place is so relaxing!" I say. "Thank you dad. For everything." Dad's smile gets bigger, but soon fades, as he starts to look confused.

"Are you okay?" he asked.

"Yeah, I'm fine. I guess." I answer. "I just keep... I don't know how to say it. I just keep *feeling* Eleanor." Dad gives me a puzzled look, so I add a quick, "Forget it, it's fine."

"No, don't forget it, what do you mean?" He responds, looking even more confused.

"Everywhere I go, I can't help but imagine Eleanor, it's kind of my way of coping. But today, it started to feel real," I start. "I know it sounds stupid, but I feel like she's here with me," I say. I brace for some sort of 'she's not here, it's all in your head.' from dad, but instead he says,

"First of all, you *never* sound stupid to me. Secondly, I know it can feel like that. I had the same thing when mom died. Do you really believe she's here though?"

"No, I don't. But it's still weird, as if I wouldn't be surprised to just see her walk up to me and start talking," I respond. Dad pauses, and looks at me in an understanding way. He gives a little nod, then says,

"Why don't we go up to the room and get ready for dinner. If you have anything more, ever, that you need to talk about; I'm here."

"Thanks dad, that sounds good," I say. As we get out of the pool and start walking back up to the room, I feel all of the imaginations of Eleanor start to slip away. The whole walk to the hotel room, as I get dressed, as my dad and I leave for dinner, even as we get seated and order; no odd imaginations of Eleanor. I haven't seen her, I haven't heard her, I haven't even been thinking about her since the pool. But as the plates of food hit the table, she was *there*. There was even food on the table for her. An extra chair. But I know it isn't real. Tears beginning to form in my eyes, I tell Dad,

"I'm going to the bathroom, I'll be right back." He looks at me like I'm crazy.

"Are you okay?" He asks me, as I walk away quickly. I open the bathroom door, and the tears fall hard and fast. I start to spiral, and I can't stop. I have to have the patience Eleanor didn't have, and I have to make the call. First ring, nothing. Second ring, *nothing*. This is where Eleanor gave up. Third ring...

"*Stay calm.*" A muffled voice says. The tears turn into sobs at the memory of the answerer when Ellie jumped. "*You will be okay. I can help. Just stay calm.*"

"Hi." I say, trying not to let my crying show.

"*What is your current situation?*" The girl on the phone says. She sounds like she's about my age, maybe 16? 17? A little older than me, but not much.

"Well, I'm in a restaurant bathroom in Hawaii. And my friend killed herself a couple days ago," I told the girl.

"I am so sorry. That must be so difficult for you. Just remember, she would want you to live. She would want you to have the most amazing life you possibly could. Keep living, for her." The girl responded.

"What's your name?" I ask her.

"My name is Ellanor." She says. I want to scream, but I just keep crying. Harder. Faster.

"Ellanor, I think you just saved my life," I told her, trying not to scream. *Ellanor.* Her name is *Ellanor.* What she had said before might have turned my thoughts, but her name just saved my life.

"Are you okay?" Ellanor says.

"Yea, I'm okay now. But my best friend, the one who died a couple of days ago, her name was Eleanor. That saved me." I cry.

"That seems almost impossible. That's amazing." She breathes, and I think I hear her sniffle a few times.

"Thank you so much Ellanor. I have to go." I tell her.

"Thank you for calling, I'm so glad I could help." She answers. As I hang up, I decide to just sit in the bathroom and cry for a little while. I text Dad, trying not to cause a scene, and tell him to meet me out front. I tell him to get our food in takeout boxes, and I tell him we have to leave. As soon as he gets out, I cry to him.

"Dad. We have to go home," I say.

"It's okay honey, we can go home. I'll get a flight. It's okay." He says, as he consoles me.

At the hotel, we start to pack up. Dad finally thinks I look stable enough, and he asks, "Why exactly do we have to leave tomorrow?"

"I..." I start, scared that Dad will be mad at me if I tell him. "I called the suicide help hotline, because I was feeling really weird. And I don't know why, I don't know how, but the girl who picked up; her name was Ellanor." I feel the tears come back, but I shut them out. I'm going to live the rest of my life well. For Eleanor.

"Oh, honey. I'm so sorry." He says. I'm so surprised he's not mad, or confused.

"Really, I think it was for the better. She told me that Eleanor would want me to live out my life well, and it was like Eleanor herself was reaching out and telling me that." I answer. I know this pain will go away. Someday I will live a day without thinking about this tragedy. But I will never forget my best friend.

3 YEARS LATER

Aurelia Ling   September 24, 2027

Hey again, diary! I haven't written in three years. Since Eleanor's death, I've decided to dedicate myself to helping people in her situation. It's my birthday today. I'm turning 18. I'm celebrating today with my amazing dad, and my best friend Ellanor, from the Suicide Hotline. We both work at the teen line. I feel so fulfilled every time someone calls and I help them. My 18th birthday is very special. It marks 3 years working for the hotline. Now, I'm a little old now for diaries, so this will be my last entry. Bye Diary!

FOREVER. :)

About the Author

Frances Heethuis is 12 years old, in 7th grade, and goes to City High/Middle School. Frances loves to write and someday wants to either be a singer/songwriter or a writer. Some of the things Frances loves are swimming, family, diving, friends and singing. Her favorite singer is Noah Kahan, and her favorite writer is Alan Gratz or Shannon Messenger. While writing *Suicide Hotline, Make the Call*, she knew she had to tread lightly with the subject. Suicide is something that is very sad but needs to be known about, so Frances took a risk. She hopes you enjoy *Suicide Hotline, Make the Call*.

Youth Published Finalist

The Present
Kayla Simons

White specks of snow fell from the cloudy skies. Piling up on each other to create mountains of white fluff. A pine tree, covered in colorful lights, with boxes of all shapes and sizes slid underneath it. The fireplace mantel had oversized socks dangling from it. Each one with a different cursive initial on it. The sun was rising, causing the sky to turn magnificent colors, yet it kept snowing. An alarm went off in the house, disturbing the eerie silence and ringing out. The children shot from their beds, their feet thumping on the ground as they ran to sit around the tree. All I did was tilt my head, scratch my ear, and wait.

"Merry Christmas, Queen!" I was instantly scooped up and held closely to the youngest child's chest. He squeezed me until I let out a small yip of hurt.

"Put her down!" the middle child exclaimed, rushing over to save me from the choking grip of the youngest, "You're choking her." The middle child reached out her hands, trying to save it from the grasp of the youngest. He yanked me away quickly before anyone could snatch me away. The two started to fight and argue over me. It was quickly settled as the parents walked into the room.

"If neither of you can agree on who will hold her, put her down." the father's voice boomed. The middle child sighed and slowly went to sit next to her older sister.

"May we start opening the gifts?" the oldest questioned from her position on the couch. The child who was holding me loosened their grip a tad and I breathed a sigh of relief. "Dad and I have one gift for all three of you, but then we must eat breakfast. I don't think the gift can wait." the mother chuckled to herself as the father went to fetch the gift from their room.

"Ooh! What is it?" the youngest finally dropped me to clap his hands together. "That would ruin the surprise of gifts, wouldn't it, Teddy?" the mother bopped him on the nose as I plopped down next to the two of them. Theodore, the youngest, bent down to pick me up again, but I scurried away before his chubby hands could land on me.

"Come back Queen, I promise I won't hurt you." Theodore stuck his fingers into his mouth, drool falling down his face and onto the red and green onesie he was wearing. I let out a tiny bark to let him know I was not in fact going back into his arms.

"Leave Queen alone, Teddy. She doesn't look like she wants to play right now." the mother pulled him away gently, "Daddy should almost be back with your gift." as if on cue, he arrived right then. His arms were full, holding a big gift. It was a basic box with a lid, the wrapping paper had little Christmas trees over it. And a big, red, shiny bow was stuck to the top of it.

The father put the present in the middle of the family room. Theodore fell down to his knees and started crawling towards it. The middle child, Grace, carefully went to go examine it. Followed by the oldest, Noel. The father pulled out his phone and started recording them. I ran over to the three children, my tail wagging, happily barking, as I plopped down in the middle of Grace and Noel.

"Can we open it?" Theodore looked eagerly up at his father. The father nodded enthusiastically, his thumb pressing the record button. Theodore started tearing at the packaging, trying to get his little hands to slide open the package. Noel swooped in and helped him, lifting up the lid and throwing it on the ground beside her. I sat back, waiting to see the present that the children were to grab.

"Oh my goodness!" Noel shrieked with excitement. She reached down into the large box, wrapping her arms delicately around the object. Grace peered into the gift, and instantly ran to hug her father, knocking him down. She got up and repeated the same to her mother. I watched, curious about what they were excited about. I didn't have to wait for very long.

Noel pulled out a tiny puppy. It had a golden coat, and big, large eyes. Its paws were huge for its body, and its tail was wagging so hard it was repeatedly smacking Noel's hands.

"A puppy!" Theodore reached out his hands, opening and shutting them, a signal for I want it . "Thank you!" Noel hugged the golden furred puppy close to her chest. She closed her eyes, breathing in the smell of the new puppy. My heart dropped as I watched the family, my family turn all of their attention to the new puppy Noel held in her arms. I let out a tiny bark, and the puppy's head turned to my direction instantly, but everyone else didn't see that.

"What shall we name it?" the mother was sitting on the floor now, next to her children, looking at the puppy with so much love and happiness in her eyes.

"How about Belle?" Grace's eyes lit up, "Like a Christmas bell?"

"Eh," Noel held up the puppy, examining it. I shrunk away. *Everyone was forgetting me* . Even the puppy- who was now looking and examining all the family members.

"What about Candy, like a candy cane?" the mother questioned, reaching out to stroke the soft fur of the new puppy.

"I love that!" Noel nodded to herself, a smile blooming on her face, "Welcome Candy." she stroked Candy softly on the head. Candy let out a small yip, wagging her tail even more.

The father took something out of his pocket. A small, red color, with a gold bell dangling off it. He handed it to Noel, who still had the puppy in her arms. This time she was cradling it like a baby, Candy's head resting in the crook of one arm, and her wagging tail laying in the other. Noel unclipped the buckle on the collar, wrapping it softly around Candy's neck, and clicking it back together with a satisfying snap.

"Let's show Candy around the house!" Grace stood up excitedly, followed by Noel and Theodore. My ears perked up, and I started to bound after them as they went on their tour of the house. Yet they never looked back and never noticed me.

I circled the gray, fluffy bed multiple times before finally settling down. I put my head on my paws, and watched as my family played with Candy. She leaped in the air, trying to smash her tiny jaws down on the rope toy they waved around.

"Candy! Candy!" her name was called out several times from each family member, cheering her on, or trying to lead her somewhere with a toy. It's nice not being the center of attention, not being too overwhelmed, and finally being able to rest my paws. At the same time, I felt left out, sad, and a little upset that my family forgot about me. The mother came and sat down on the leather sofa, which was towering above me. Her eyes fluttered around the room, looking at Candy, her kids, her husband, and then finally landing on me.

"Are you sleepy, Queen?" she pushed herself up and off the couch, then settled down next to my bed. Her smooth, yet cold hand stroked my head and I felt my tail start to wag. My ears perked up and I became a tiny bit happy once again. I let out a tiny bark of gratitude, lifting my head. The mother started to scratch my ears, and I once again felt my tail start to wag even more. The tiny window with the lines through it that let anyone see in or out of the house showed that once again the world was being covered in a thin blanket of white snow. I let my head drop again, but the mother kept stroking it. My eyelids drooped down, growing heavy and tired. My brain began to power off as I slowly went to sleep, but it was rudely interrupted. A tiny, cool, rough tongue brushed back a little fur on the top of my head. My eyelids burst open as I glared at the tiny puppy who decided to lick me. I let out a tiny growl, not to scare Candy, but just to warn her to leave me alone.

Candy bounced back a couple of puppy paws, and let out a whimper. Grace was quick to shout at me. "Queen! Candy was doing nothing wrong, leave her alone." she ran to gather the whimpering puppy in her arms.

"I believe Queen was trying to sleep and Candy woke her, there is no reason to blame her," the mother quickly spoke. All Grace did was shrug, and the three children went back to playing with the puppy, the father sitting close by. I closed my eyelids once again, and really did go to sleep that time.

The snow had vanished, and fresh, healthy looking green leaves had replaced the bare branches. Instead of all gathering in the family room to play with the Christmas gifted puppy, Candy, they gathered outside. Throwing tennis balls in the yard for her to fetch and bring back. Even I was impressed, and shocked at how much the tiny golden puppy had grown. She was practically my size now, and I've only been living there for four years. Candy ran up to me, her paws thumping on the green grass. She dropped a sticky, saliva drenched tennis ball in front of my paws. It didn't bother me, we were practically related. I picked it up in my jaws, and started running away from the little puppy. She quickly followed me, trying to bite and chomp down on my tail. I turned around to growl at her, to tell her she wasn't allowed, never allowed, to do that. Candy jumped back, a little shocked that I was barking at her, but it wasn't unusual.

"Candy! It's time to take you on a walk!" Noel came out of the house, with a red leash in her hands. She bent down next to the puppy, holding down on the golden colored clip of the leash and attaching it to Candy's matching collar. I titled, my head, waiting for my walk.

Noel and Candy started to walk off, leaving a small trail in the grass of where their feet and paws previously were. I started to bound after them, but Noel stopped me.

"Not right now, Queen. I'll take you on a walk later, alright?" she bent down to give me a tiny pat on the head. I let out a tiny whimper, only to be patted on the head once again. *I didn't want head pats, I just wanted to be loved again.* I plopped down in the grass as Noel and Candy walked off. Noel's hand was firmly gripped onto Candy's leash, and Candy led the way. I looked down at the grass, distracting myself from anything but seeing

Candy obviously receiving more love and attention than me. The best thing for a distraction I could find was a small little flower. It was smashed, most likely from where a human or animal had once stepped on. I scooped my little paw underneath it, helping it stand nice and tall again. I hope that would be me someday, standing up, tall, happy, and proud once again.

Noel and Grace had taken Candy somewhere, probably for a stroll around the neighborhood, and to a store to get a pup cup after. I was sitting in my fluffy bed, where I spend most of my days. My head was resting on my paws and I was trying to sleep. My brain didn't like that idea. It kept imaging, replaying, and thinking about how nobody seemed to love me anymore. I whimpered, and whimpered, rolling around and trying to fall asleep. Soft pitter-patters of the carpet being flattened by feet floated to my ears. I could never fall asleep without someone trying to interrupt me. My ears flattened to my head, and I whimpered once more until I could see the person turning the corner.

"Oh, my poor baby. They're not giving you enough love since that Christmas puppy showed up, eh?" the mother crouched down beside my bed. I whimpered a little, to show I understood, that *she* understood.

"I'll make them take you on a walk as soon as they get home, don't worry nobody leaves out my precious Queen." she reached her hand out to scratch my ears, making my tail wag the most it has in days. A couple of minutes flew by, but I held onto them like precious memories. Making sure they will always stick to my memory. Finally being noticed and loved- and by the mother of the family. She stood up and kissed me on my furry head. I looked up at her, making my puppy eyes. The lovable puppy eyes that made the family go, *"that's the one"* while walking through the animal shelter hallways, looking at each puppy behind the steel bars.

"I'm sorry baby-" the mother was cut off with the interruption of the doorbell chimes ringing throughout the house. My ears instantly perked up, and I *sprang* up from the fluffy, cloud-like bed. I went bounding for the front door, quickly followed by the mother, giggling and snorting like a pig as she chased after me.

I halted at the door, my paws sliding on the carpet, and making it roll forward and wrinkle like a cloth in the washing machine. The mother slid up behind me, almost tripping over my body, but catching herself on the gray front door.

"Oh, my bad." she bent down for a little to give me a pat on the head, rising back up quickly to unlock the door and twist the handle.

She smoothed her hair, calming down the frizziness of the brown strands, and opened the door. I padded over to sit by her feet. In walked Noel, Grace, and Candy. Candy's head was held high, her paws confidently leading the way, her leash firmly gripped by Noel.

"You two should take Queen for a walk!" the mother exclaimed with a tone of firmness in her voice, gently shutting the door behind her. Noel bent down to unclip the leash from the collar of the puppy.

"No thanks." Grace skipped to the family room, most likely to dig out some sort of chew toy to play with Candy.

"Yes, thank you very much." the mother pulled off the light pink collar off the hooks by the front door, at the same time Noel hung up the red one. She walked after Grace, her steps loud yet growing quieter. She rested her hand on Grace's shoulders, turning her around and handing her the pink collar.

"Nobody gives her much love anymore, she's still our dog. We love our dogs *equally*." she glanced over her shoulder back to where Noel waited by the front door. With a heavy sigh, Noel picked me up. My ears perk up and I feel my tail start wagging. "Here, I'll do it, Mom's right." she walked over to the spot where the mother and middle child were arguing, she reached out her hand to Grace, waiting for her to hand over the leash. Reluctantly, she did. Noel bent down to clip it to my matching collar, walking me to the front door, opening it, and walking out. This time, I held my head high, paws leading me confidently, and the leash held firmly.

"Queen," I spun around to look at the voice who called my name, "Fetch!" a pink tennis ball went flying through the air, a whooshing sound flew past my ears, and I instantly bolted after it. I heard the sound of paws thumping on the grass beside me. I looked out of the corner of my eye to see a golden dog, her ears flying backwards in the wind, her pink tongue hanging out, and her figure towering over me racing for the same ball. We propelled ourselves forward, challenging ourselves to see who could snatch up the ball first. Candy flung herself ahead of me, rolling over and over until her jaws could clamp around the pink tennis ball.

"Candy!" Noel giggled, racing after us, her hair trailing behind her, "That was for Queen." she caught up quickly to where we sat, our heads tilted at her. Falling to her knees, she wrestled Candy for the tennis ball, snapping it out of her grasp. Candy let out large barks, her tail thumping on the grass next to her. Noel's hair was spread out all over the grass, her arms in the air. Candy laid her head on Noel's chest and I went to join the two. The rest of the family was nearby, sitting at a picnic table. The mother got up and snapped a picture of us three with us. Laughter filled the air, and the last time I felt this happy was a long time ago.

My tongue fell out of my mouth as Noel started scratching my belly, followed by doing the same to Candy but with the other hand.

"I love you." Noel whispered into my ear, "I love both of you." Those three words I have been waiting to hear forever. I snuggled closer to Noel, my tail thumping against her side. I let out four happy barks, *"I love you too."*

About the Author

Kayla Simons is a student from Armada, MI. Kayla took an interest in writing and reading at a very young age. She started a writing club in elementary school and joined the school newspaper in middle school, becoming one of the co-editors. While she loves all genres of literature, fantasy is her favorite to read and write. She is honored to be part of the Write Michigan contest and is thankful for the opportunity to share her story with others.Youth Published Finalist

A Friend to Follow
Jesca Westra

The rising sun shone brightly between the buildings of Shadwell, on London's east end, making Arthur's azure eyes shine and his light brown hair glisten. "Good morning, lad," shouted the fruit stand attendant, as she stacked her produce for the day. "You'd better step lively or you'll be late for school!" Her words interrupted his daydreaming. "Don't worry," he replied. "I have not been late yet!"

The truth was, however, that Arthur frequently was late, especially when he found himself daydreaming about dogs. What made his eyes truly sparkle with delight was the sight of a dog, any dog. His love for dogs burned even hotter than the sun, and this morning he had found himself daydreaming after the butcher's dog, Milly, greeted him with a friendly bark, as she did each morning. How he would have loved to take Milly to school with him to bark at his teacher and then home to snuggle with him in his room and to eat his vegetables secretly under the table.

Arthur was an only child, and his father was away at war. His mother was a kind woman who did all that she could for Arthur. Yet, despite his constant nagging, she would not let him get a dog, because they lived in a small, fourth-floor flat. His walk to school each day took him past little shops and narrow alleys, which provided him with many possibilities to be distracted, especially if he spotted a dog along the way.

Arthur made it to school on time, but just barely. As he walked into class, his teacher, Miss Milson, was checking attendance and looked over to see Arthur sliding into his desk chair. Arthur smiled innocently as he took out his books to begin class.

The first class of the day was arithmetic. Arthur enjoyed maths, so time passed quickly. Then, it was time for history. Arthur's mind began to drift, but he was quickly brought back to reality by the sound of the air raid siren. His teacher announced, "Ok, class, it's time for another drill." She rounded them all up and led them to the safe room. There, they were required to sit quietly until the "All clear" was announced. Arthur got bored easily during these drills, and so did most of the other children. His mind often wandered during this time, as he thought about what his father was doing at that moment. He wondered if his father was visiting wonderful, exotic places.

The drill took up the rest of history class, and then it was time for lunch. Goodness ,was Arthur hungry! He quickly spotted his friend, Albert, and sat down beside him in the refectory as he unwrapped his sandwich.

"Those bomb drills sure are a waste of time," said Arthur.

"I agree," replied Albert. "We've done so many."

"Well, at least we will be prepared if something actually happens."

"I guess," said Albert, not really thinking too much about it.

Arther finished his sandwich and went to his next class. The day lagged on, and Arthur went from class to class with no further drills or other excitement.

Finally, the day ended, and Arthur excitedly bounded out the door of the school. As he was walking home from school with Albert, he spotted a greyhound searching for food in the middle of the street. Arthur thought she was beautiful, despite her mud speckled fur and paws. "Here, girl," he called. The dog raised her head, startled, but Arthur brought out his leftover sandwich from school dinner. Soon, the dog started walking towards him.

"Aren't you just the sweetest girl?" he cooed. "I wonder if mother will let me keep you?"

"What are you doing with that stray dog?" asked Albert disdainfully.

"I'm taking her home," replied Arthur, excitedly. "I'll name her Blaze, because she looks fast and fiery!"

"You'd better give her a bath if you are to have any chance of convincing your mother to keep her."

"Gladly," replied Arthur.

He walked home with Blaze, using his school suspenders as a leash. She walked gently behind him. She seemed to sense he was a friend.

When Arthur got home, he brought Blaze to the back of his building and gave her a bath, using a hose, and cleaned her up as much as possible. He then snuck her upstairs, past his neighbors on the ground floor, up to the flat he shared with his mother. He brought her into the kitchen and made her a peanut butter sandwich. While she was gobbling the food down, he heard his mother opening the front door to the flat.

Arthur knew the time had come for him to ask his mom if he could keep his new dog. As his mother walked into the kitchen, she suddenly shrieked as she noticed Blaze.

"Arthur! Where did that dog come from?" she exclaimed.

Arthur replied, "When two dogs love each other very, very much..."

His mother interrupted him quickly, "No, Arthur! For the last time, you cannot have a dog. We have no room in this house. I am sorry, but you cannot keep her!"

Arthur could not believe it. He walked her back outside, past the neighbor's doors again, and sadly said goodbye.

"I am sorry, Blaze. I would have loved to keep you. Please be safe out there."

As he let her out of his suspenders, she loped off a bit, before turning to look back. He shooed her with his hands, and she put her head down and walked away.

Days passed and Arthur could not stop thinking about his dog friend. After school one day, Arthur was playing jacks with Albert in the school yard. As they were playing, they heard the air raid sirens go off.

Arthur yelled, "We need to get to the tube! Hurry! Hurry!" They began to run. Albert was in front, and Arthur struggled to keep up with him.

"Slow down Albert!" he cried, but in the rush of fearful civilians looking for shelter, Albert was nowhere to be seen. Arthur had lost sight of him, and he had lost his bearing in finding the station.

Arthur looked around desperately searching for someone whom he knew. And he suddenly spotted someone! It was her, Blaze! She was cowering behind a dumpster, trying to escape the rush of people.

Arthur ran up to her and hugged her. But she jumped back quickly and started spinning in circles. She then nudged him to follow her.

"What are you doing, Blaze? What do you want?" said Arthur.

But Blaze just continued nudging and then leaping forward. So, Arthur moved toward her and followed when she took off.

They ran together, Arthur not knowing where she was taking him. They passed building after building, and soon they were at the tube station.

"How did you know the way? Blaze, you saved my life!" he cried.

They rushed down the stairs, and when he looked up, he saw his mother and yelled, "Mummy!" He ran up, hugged her, and explained what his loyal dog friend did. His mom was impressed and so happy he was safe. Arthur, his mother, and Blaze had to spend the night in the tube waiting for the bombing to cease. His mother comforted him, Blaze comforted his mother and him both, though she was scared. His mom was beginning to like Blaze.

In the morning, they were able to leave and go home. Arthur's mother said to him, "Arthur, you may keep Blaze IF you walk her every morning, keep her in your bed at night, and keep her clean."

"I promise I will do all those things. Thanks, mom!"

Arthur made sure Blaze had everything she could wish for, and from then on, they became best friends and always looked out for each other. They had many adventures to await them.

About the Author

Jesca Westra is a sixth grader at Trinitas Classical School. She received a gold medal for the National Latin Exam and a silver medal for the National Myth Exam in 5th grade. She adores dogs and has rescued two, Jago and Julep. In her free time, Jesca enjoys crafts, including making models with her dad and painting with her mom. Jesca loves most sports but particularly likes tennis, flag football and playing basketball with her brother, Jude. Jesca loves history and fiction.

About Write Michigan

The Write Michigan Short Story Contest began in 2012 as a dream.

Kent District Library Director Lance Werner envisioned libraries and publishers working together to highlight the efforts of Michigan writers via an independently published book.

Since then, Write Michigan has become a celebrated annual event that invites Michigan residents of all ages to showcase their storytelling talents.

Organized by Kent District Library and Schuler Books, the contest aims to foster a love for writing and provide a platform for local authors to gain recognition. Over the years, it has grown in popularity, attracting hundreds of entries each year from aspiring writers across the state.

Participants are divided into three categories: youth, teens and adults, ensuring that writers of all ages have the opportunity to compete on a level playing field. The contest features a rigorous judging process, with entries evaluated by a panel of experts as well as through public voting.

Winners in each category receive cash prizes and the honor of having their stories published in an anthology by Chapbook Press, which is available for purchase at Schuler Books.

The Write Michigan Short Story Contest not only celebrates the art of storytelling, but also builds a vibrant literary community in Michigan. It offers various writing events and workshops throughout the year, including the popular Days of Learning, which provide valuable resources and support for writers. The contest has become a cornerstone of Michigan's literary scene, inspiring countless individuals to share their unique voices and stories.

2024-2025 Judges

JOSH BOERS

Joshua Boers has published short stories and poetry in *Procrastinating Writers United, The MockingOwl Roost* and *Infinity Wanderers.* He also won the Judge's Choice award in the 2024 Write Michigan Short Story Contest. By day, he is an editorial assistant at an indie book publisher. By night, he can generally be found reading P. G. Wodehouse novels, playing with his cat Mishka or doubling the garlic in a fried rice recipe.

ERIN HAHN

Erin Hahn is the author of the young adult novels *You'd Be Mine, More Than Maybe, Never Saw You Coming* and *Even if it Breaks Your Heart,* as well as the adult romances *Built to Last* and *Friends Don't Fall in Love.* Romance is her vibe, grunge is her soundtrack and fall is her signature color. She fell for her flannel-clad college sweetheart the very first day of school, and together they have two hilarious kids who keep her humble. She lives outside Ann Arbor, Michigan.

JIM C. HINES

Jim C. Hines is the author of the *Magic ex Libris* series, the *Princess* series of fairy tale retellings, the humorous *Goblin Quest* trilogy and the Fable Legends tie-in *Blood of Heroes*. He also won the 2012 Hugo Award for Best Fan Writer. His latest novel is *Terminal Peace*, book three in the humorous science fiction *Janitors of the Post-Apocalypse* trilogy. He lives in mid-Michigan with his family.

KENDRA R. MCNEIL

Kendra R. McNeil is an independent bookseller and owner of the bookshop We Are LIT based in Grand Rapids, MI. Her work focuses on creating a culture around books in the community. McNeil served as a returning juror for the annual Scholastic Art & Writing Awards, where she reviewed work submissions from students in the West Central Michigan Region in journalism and novel writing. She is a lifelong reader lover of books, and avid traveler. In addition to operating We Are LIT, McNeil enjoys outdoor adventures and is a hobbyist nature and wildlife photographer. McNeil holds a degree in legal studies from Davenport University and is a proud member of the American Booksellers Association.

JAY BARON NICORVO

Jay Baron Nicorvo's true-crime memoir, *Best Copy Available*, won the AWP Award selected by Geoff Dyer. His novel, *The Standard Grand*, landed at #8 on the Indie Next List, and his poetry collection, *Deadbeat*, debuted on the Poetry Foundation bestseller list. He lives on an old farm outside Battle Creek, Michigan with his wife, Thisbe Nissen, their son, a couple cats, a dog and a dozen chickens.

Jay's writing has been featured on NPR and PBS NewsHour. He's served as an editor at *Ploughshares* and at PEN America, and he spent years as Membership Director of the Community of Literary Magazines and Presses in NYC. A proud community-college graduate, Jay's taught at Eckerd College, Emerson College and Western Michigan University. He's also stocked the toilet paper aisle of a Winn-Dixie, clerked at a drugstore, solicited donations for the Florida Police Athletic League and waited tables at a fondue restaurant, a steak house and a French bistro. He was most recently a guest artist at the Cornell College low-residency program in creative writing. Find Jay at www.nicorvo.net.

ANDY ROGERS

Andy Rogers is a ghostwriter and editor. He's the author of eight books and has contributed to numerous others. His story, *Archived*, won the Reader's Choice Award for the 2013 Write Michigan Short Story contest. He has since published short fiction in *Splickety Magazine, Catapult Magazine and* DailyScienceFiction.com and elsewhere. Learn more at www.andyrogersbooks.com.

JOY WALCZAK

Joy wrote and illustrated her first book in second grade, *Fun with Rubber Bands,* but has yet to publish it. There are many unfinished works she hopes to one day complete. She is motivated to do so by authors of all ages who have enriched her life in many ways. Through nearly three decades in media, marketing and communications, writing has always been an integral part of Joy's life's work and creative expression. To inspire others to read and write is a great privilege, and she's grateful for the opportunity to be part of the Write Michigan experience.

JANE ZWART

Jane Zwart teaches at Calvin University, where she also co-directs the Calvin Center for Faith & Writing. Her poems have appeared in *Poetry, Ploughshares* and *North American Review,* as well as other journals and magazines. Along with Timothy Liu, she co-edits book reviews for *Plume,* and her own reviews have been published in a number of places, including *The Los Angeles Review of Books.*

Acknowledgments

Over the last thirteen years, the Write Michigan Short Story Contest has helped authors share their stories with the world.

We extend our heartfelt gratitude to the esteemed judges of the 2024-2025 Write Michigan Short Story Contest: Josh Boers, Erin Hahn, Jim C. Hines, Kendra R. McNeil, Jay Baron Nicorvo, Andy Rogers, Joy Walczak and Jane Zwart. Your dedication and expertise have been invaluable in selecting the outstanding stories featured in this anthology. We are also deeply honored to have Janyre Tromp as our Keynote Author, whose insights and inspiration have enriched this year's contest.

This anthology would not have been possible without the generous support of our sponsors: Schuler Books, Meijer, Kent District Library, Traverse Area District Library and Bayliss Public Library. Your contributions have helped us nurture the creative spirit within our community and provide a platform for local writers to shine.

Thanks also to the Write Michigan Committee for tirelessly organizing, promoting and bringing fun to the contest: Brad Baker, Amber Elder, Keeva Filipek, Randy Goble, Janice Greer, Josh Mosey, Lauren Hagerman Tekelly, Deb Schultz, Remington Steed and Katie Zuidema.

Lance Warner, Executive Director of Kent District Library, and Bill and Cecile Fehsenfeld, owners of Schuler Books, have been steadfast champions of this project since day one.

Our appreciation goes out to artist Adolfo Valle for providing us with the beautiful Write Michigan artwork. Everyone loves the turtle. See more of Adolfo's work at adolfovallestudios.com.

We are immensely thankful to the public who submitted their stories, sharing their unique voices and perspectives. Our heartfelt appreciation goes out to the volunteers who tirelessly read and evaluated the entries, ensuring a fair and thorough judging process. Finally, we express our gratitude to the readers and buyers of this anthology. Your support not only celebrates the talent of local artists but also helps sustain a vibrant literary community in Michigan. Thank you for being a part of this creative journey.

Josh Mosey, Kent District Library
Pierre Camy, Schuler Books

Sponsors

SCHULER
BOOKS

Chapbook Press

Kent
District
Library

meijer

Self-Publishing Services

What are the benefits of printing your work with Schuler Books?

- This is your book.
- You'll receive one-on-one support
- Since you sign a non-exclusive contract with us, you may pursue any other publishing venture that you choose.
- You retain all rights to the printed work, and you have complete control over layout, content and design.
- No minimums for private printings. You may print one copy or as many as you want. If you choose the global distribution option you will need to place a first order of 50 copies.
- You retain rights for non-exclusive distribution and may sell books printed by Schuler Books and Chapbook Press through any avenue.
- Modifications are allowed at any time, for an additional fee.
- You set the book price.

What we need to print your book

2 print-ready PDF files: one for the book and one for the cover, formatted the way you want them to look. We will upload your files and print a paperback or hardcover edition of your book on high quality (archival) paper and a full-color glossy cover, or optional matte cover, in a range of sizes from 4"x6" to 8.5"x11" (portrait) or 11"x8.5" (landscape). Please check with us about the trim size to make sure we can work with it.

We can help you get there

We can help as much or as little as needed in each area of making your book a reality.

- Global distribution print and digital package: your title (in print or as an eBook) will be available for purchase to over 45,000 global retailers, and their customers. The eBook will be available for more than 70 different eReaders including Amazon Kindle, Apple iBookstore, Barnes&Noble NOOK, Kobo, Sony, etc.) Bookstores and retailers around the world will be able to order your book for their customers. First order of at least 50 copies. Additional orders (minimum quantity of 10), require a three week notice.
- Epub Conversion: $1.00 per page (page count is based on the total number of pages in your bookblock)
  - Conversion will take three weeks.

Chapbook Press

Chapbook Press

	Standard Package Private Printing $260 Plus Production Costs	Chapbook Press Publinshing Global Distribution Book only $620 BW or $670 color Plus Production Costs	Chapbook Press Publinshing Global Distribution Book + eBook $750 BW or $800 color Plus Production Costs
Maximum Print Run	Unlimited	Unlimited	Unlimited
Page Maximum	More than 1000 pages	More than 1000 pages	More than 1000 pages
Personal Consultation	30 Minutes	60 Minutes	60 Minutes
Email Support	Included	Included	Included
PDF Review	Yes	Yes	Yes
Proof Copy	1 Proof Copy	1 Proof Copy	1 Proof Copy
PDF Upload	Includes initial upload +1 Re-upload	Includes initial upload +1 Re-upload	Includes initial upload +1 Re-upload
Cover	Basic Template Cover or one hour of cover design	Basic Template Cover or one hour of cover design	Basic Template Cover or one hour of cover design
Saved for Re-prints	Yes	Yes	Yes
ISBN/Barcode	No	1 (paperback)	2 (Paperback + eBook)
Library of Congress Reg.	No	Yes	Yes
Books in Print Reg.	No	Yes	Yes
For sale at Schuler Books	No	Yes	Yes
For sale at SchulerBooks.com	No	Yes	Yes
Production Costs	Ask for a quote.	Ask for a quote.	eBook conversion $1.00 per page
Color Interior	Ask for a quote.	Ask for a quote.	

A la Carte Services

Transcribing: $126 deposit, $42 per hour
Coaching/Consulting: $60 deposit, $60 per hour
Manuscript evaluation: $300
Content/Copy Editing: $54 per hour, $162 deposit
Proofreading: $126 deposit, $42 per hour
Scanning: $60 deposit, $60 per hour
Page Layout: Based on a quote
Custom Cover Design: $120 deposit, $60 per hour

PDF Alterations (re-uploads): $35 (+ price of proof copy)
ISBN & barcode acquisition: $120
Library of Congress Registration: $60
Additional consultation time: $60 per hour
Hardcover Binding: Ask for a quote.

For more information visit SchulerBooks.com
Want to talk to someone? Call us today at 616-942-7330 x 558,
or email us at: printondemand@schulerbooks.com or pierre@schulerbooks.com

www.ingramcontent.com/pod-product-compliance
Lightning Source LLC
Chambersburg PA
CBHW071426300726

48976CB00004B/1255